AB TERRA 2022

AB TERRA 2022

EDITED BY YEN OOI · AND · DAWN OSTLUND

Cover design by Dawn Ostlund.

Published in the United States by Ab Terra Books, an imprint of Brain Mill Press.

Print ISBN 978-1-948559-84-3

EPUB ISBN 978-1-948559-85-0

MOBI ISBN 978-1-948559-86-7

CONTENTS

WHEN I WAS A CHILD, I OWNED A BOOK CALLED *The Universe*. IT WAS FILLED WITH PICTURES OF STARS AND GALAXIES, DEPICTED IN VIVID COLOUR. I DON'T know how many hours I spent poring over that book, but it was one of the very earliest inspirations for my science fiction stories. What is sometimes referred to in the genre as *sensawunda,* or "sense of wonder"—that feeling of fascination and (sometimes humbling) awe we feel when we encounter something utterly unknown and utterly unlike ourselves—lies at the core of what draws us to the genre. It reflects our hunger to understand our place in the universe. Who we are and, above all, where we are headed or have the potential to go.

But despite, or perhaps because of, this, science fiction has always served as a reminder of how much we have in common with our fellow humans here on earth, regardless of our myriad cultures and religions, our varied histories and perspectives. Though on the surface science fiction seems to ask us to look outward—up at those colourful galaxies that occupied so much of my youth—the reality is, the genre forces us to look more deeply within ourselves. The truths it has to tell us—that we humans are a single species on a single rock, and that we have only begun to scratch the surface of understanding our universe—unite us.

I feel this sense of unity is vital at the current time, a time of increasing political and economic division. To survive as a species, we have to work together. As we grapple with the environmental, financial, and civic challenges that face us, science fiction offers us a way to understand what is happening and to imagine alternatives. Though this genre often shows us the worst possibilities of humanity, it also reminds us that the power to change course lies within us as a species. I can think of nothing that better enables me to process and express what troubles me about the present day than engaging with science fiction in all its varied forms. Even though it so often looks to the future or to other worlds, few genres are more reflective of the preoccupations of the zeitgeist. Science fiction has always taken the fears, hopes, and injustices of the present and extrapolated from them.

And yet... despite being a genre that requires us to question, to push back, to imagine deeply, science fiction has been disappointingly conservative in the range of voices it chooses to champion. But things are, slowly, starting to improve. Our genre is far, far richer now than it was thirty, or even ten, years ago. Voices that once didn't have a platform are beginning to be heard. There is still a lot of work to be done. But in order for science fiction to reach its potential—and for me, science fiction has always been about potential, about what could be—the genre must embrace the full range of voices that are out there waiting to be heard. This won't happen by accident; it will happen through the conscious choices of individuals: of the writers, editors, publishers, and readers of science fiction works. We must all make a conscious effort to read more widely, to seek out new voices and historically marginalized voices, to expand our horizons.

Back in the days when I used to stare at pictures of the universe, I knew I wanted to write science fiction and fantasy, but I didn't think it would ever be a reality. People who looked like me, who sounded like me, who came from my social background, didn't get to share our dreams or tell stories that extrapolate from our own experiences. I yearned to apply that sensawunda to my own life. What changed for me, as I got older, was discovering that voices like mine did exist in the genre: they just needed a platform. That is why anthologies such as *Ab Terra* are so vital. For our genre, our species, to reach our potential, we have to do so together—all of us. Here in this collection,

you will find stories of memory and consciousness,
of transformation and belonging, and, above all, of
shared wonder and shared kinship, two concepts that
lie at the heart of what makes us human.

M. H. Ayinde
London, April 2023

AB TERRA 2022

MEMORY AND AUGURY - BY SORAMIMI HANAREJIMA

1. VESTIGIAL TELEPATHY

I WAKE UP OUT OF A DREAM THAT MUST HAVE BEEN someone's actual experience of inspecting memories—a procedure too meticulous to have been fabricated by my mind. The handling of recollections in that lab facility was so incredibly thorough, with rigorous high-tech scrutiny applied to the emotions and judgment layered over the core of each memory— that past moment it encapsulates.

I shift my gaze from the beige ceiling to the early summer sunlight on the maple tree outside the bedroom window to my left. The dream recedes from my attention, and I try to remember the last time I had this kind of dream. But my mind goes all the way back to the first time—when I sat up in bed with the visceral certainty that the dream lingering in my thoughts had to be about something real, because it was more vivid than any dream I'd had before, the details in it almost palpable and unlikely to have been invented by my imagination.

In that dream, I was at a construction site, a stretch of road where a crew was hard at work with heavy-duty equipment. My job there was to spray silence from a tank strapped to my back, muffling the metallic percussion of jackhammering and aggressive scraping of excavation. Which, strangely, hadn't been that loud to begin with. Maybe I was wearing earplugs or had sprayed silence into my ears earlier—a safety measure necessary for those responsible for making the city quieter.

During breakfast that morning, I told Mom about the dream, then asked, "Do people actually spray silence to quiet down noisy things?"

"They do," she answered and—after a sip of coffee—added, "just not here. We have a strong undercurrent of natural silence flowing through this valley, and people are good about doing things quietly and setting up sound barriers so that silence doesn't get polluted."

"But if I didn't know that people spray silence, how did I have a dream about it? How can I dream about something I've never seen or heard of?"

"Ah, right," Mom said, then put down her mug and folded her arms on the kitchen table. "That was probably a dream of someone in real life working their job. Your sleeping mind connecting to that person's actual experience while it was happening. I used to have dreams like that at your age. It's normal, just your mind's way of reaching out into the world, meeting others that are also reaching out, sometimes reaching into faraway places in other time zones."

I thought that would be it—Mom's explanation putting this dream behind me so we'd go on with life as usual—but I kept having dreams about going to the noisy parts of a city to quiet things down. Always from the perspective of the same person who wore an old watch, its weathered leather band wrapped around her slender wrist, the position of the watch's hour and minute hands against the pearlescent dial frequently consulted, seemingly for the sake of staying on some schedule or keeping track of how time was being spent. For some reason, my mind was repeatedly reaching out to her—or her experiences insisted on entering my sleep. In one, she drove a tanker truck to a factory and pumped silence into the ventilation system, then drove to a fancy restaurant and refilled its reservoir of silence. Several nights later, she was resupplying the tanker at a silence refinery that looked as if it were made entirely of stainless steel pipes. And though I saw everything from her perspective, it felt like I was tagging along as she did her job, watching while she took care of tasks in this ongoing series of dreams.

"Well, that happens," Mom said when I told her, again over breakfast, that I'd had the same kind of dream for the fifth time. "It's uncommon, and probably means there's something that gets your mind and this other person's mind to connect. Does it bother you?"

"No. But what if it did? What if I—my mind kept connecting to a bully who's always picking on other kids?"

"Your mind would eventually move on to someone else or go back to dreaming made-up things," Mom said. "And if it didn't, that usually means something. Like your mind hopes the bully will stop being mean or wants to see what the consequences will be. If you kept having unpleasant dreams about a bully harassing other kids, you could take an amnesiac to prevent those dreams from being part of your long-term memories."

"Oh, okay," I said and left it at that.

There was nothing else to ask Mom, because I was satisfied with that last answer. More than satisfied, in fact—relieved, set at ease by the knowledge that there was a simple solution if somehow my mind couldn't help itself and ended up fixated on something upsetting.

But I should have known then that the peacekeeper was probably trying to share her perspective, one that showed how a society relies on imported silence—and showed me how lucky some of us are to live in naturally quiet places. And so, accustomed to abundant silence, my young mind latched onto that perspective, intrigued that the spraying of silence was simply an ordinary part of how a modern city was run.

I'm sure Mom had handily surmised that something along those lines was connecting me and the peacekeeper, and I'm sure she hadn't said anything about that because she wanted me to come to this realization myself. She probably hoped that in doing so I would work out some new understanding of my relationship with silence.

This morning, the realization couldn't have been more instantaneous, unfurling the moment I woke up from the dream of methodically examining memories—the meaning of the dream so obvious that I didn't bother to articulate it to myself. But I do now, to acknowledge it: I want my memories to have that fate—to someday be treated with such care, the suitable ones identified and parsed for the sake of better knowing the human condition.

I smile at this thought, even though I've already decided to take the course of action the dream was nudging me toward. Now it's time to get out into the day's abundant sunlight.

2. A NEW USE FOR OLD MEMORIES

AFTER A SET OF MEMORY RECALL TESTS, I'M BACK ON the plush sofa of the memory archive waiting room, a space that I can now see for what it is: deliberately set up to ensure comfort and thereby relaxation with its soft lighting (mostly natural through frosted glass), landscape paintings, and luxuriant ficus trees in pots with matte seafoam glaze. Together, they create a soothing atmosphere, one that really did the trick an hour ago, putting me at ease before the evaluation part of my appointment.

I barely notice the minutes passing, content to let them flow by as they will until Dr. Burndle comes in to get me. Then I follow her down the metallic hallway and into a consultation room, a small office with leafy plants in every corner and none of the equipment of the examination room we were in earlier. Each in a padded chair, we sit on opposite sides of an empty desk.

"Your memories are in good shape. Deterioration, confabulation, and backpropagation are all well within the normal ranges," she says, gaze still incisive as though she's continuing the evaluation. "And we'd like to use your memories for a new initiative. If you're interested, your memories can serve as training data to develop the personality of an AI, probably one that would go on to become a teacher, counselor, health assistant, or well-being coach."

"So the AI learns from memories … how to behave?"

"Yes. Basically, this project uses donated memories to tune artificial emotional intelligence. Would you like to hear more about that?"

"Definitely."

The desk's projector flickers on and shines a holographic flowchart between us. Leaning forward, she takes me through each step of the chart with measured enthusiasm. The first is *Input*: half a memory of a specific event is given to the AI's proto-mind. That's followed by *Output*: the AI predicts the most likely emotional response to that event. Then there's *Feedback*: the AI gets the rest of the memory, which has the actual emotional response. The AI uses that to verify or correct aes prediction and improve the accuracy of future predictions. The process is repeated for an entire set of memories.

"And the result is a model of how emotions work?" I ask.

"Yes, exactly! That model serves as the basis for how the AI thinks about people's emotions and how the AI responds to interactions with or between people. The AI's personality would be informed by yours, though the process keeps your memories entirely private. The AI can't recall them because ae wouldn't have any to recall. Similar to the way experiences we no longer remember have shaped our thinking by forming our intuition and implicit assumptions."

"Sounds promising, but wouldn't a lot be riding on my memories?"

"Your memories would be part of how the AI learns. It's akin to a child learning emotional intelligence. A little boy sees how his mother reacts to things, and, yes, he's influenced by her behavior, but he isn't destined to react as she would. He'll have other experiences that inform his relationship with emotions. Like school."

"Okay, that makes sense."

"If you let us use your memories for this project, they would likely be just one training set for the AI. That way the AI learns from a variety of people's experiences."

"Those multiple training sets make the artificial emotional intelligence more well-rounded, right?"

"Yes, exactly. We call it Synthetic Empathy, a kind of empathy synthesized from memories of various actual experiences."

Dr. Burndle turns off the projector, and the flowchart dims away.

"Take some time to think about it," she says with a smile. "When you've made your decision, let us know. No matter what you decide, we encourage you to continue forming solid memories by getting restful sleep, eating well, limiting distractions, and, for good measure, meditating."

"Sounds like things I should be doing anyway," I reply.

"Yes, activities that enhance well-being do tend to enhance the formation and maintenance of memories."

3. THE PROMISE OF MEMORY

ON MY WAY TO WORK, I WALK THROUGH THE CENTRAL wildlife corridor, its thick vegetation buffering me from the city's bustle, the quiet minutes here insulating me from the responsibilities that await me at the office—all the causal mapping that remains to be done. On this wood-chipped path along the creek, I have time to think about finally taking the kind of step that Mom took decades ago.

I never asked Mom why she became a memory donor. I never had to. I never knew a time when she wasn't enchanted by the idea of being one. In her college days, she got swept up in her generation's collective excitement after the memory donation program was announced with much fanfare—touted as a revolution in how we'd value our collective experiences. All throughout my childhood, she mentioned those days with such fondness, describing the pervasive glow of shared optimism that our lived experiences could, if we chose, contribute to humanity's comprehension of itself. We could join the ranks of bygone scholars and leaders who left their records to museums—bequeathing trunks full of journals and letters and photographs that would, in the hands of researchers, yield insights not just about the lives those documents were part of but also about life as a human being. Through the analysis of donated memories, important events could be considered from myriad perspectives: ordinary and extraordinary and everything in between. We would learn about ourselves from each other with an unprecedented granularity—all in service of greater lucidity.

Like so many of her generation, Mom—before she was Mom—was so taken by this idea of learning from all our experiences, not just those of a select few. So taken that she committed to being a donor years before my birth, pledging memories of a motherhood that hadn't yet begun, to a fledgling paradigm shift in humanity's comprehension of itself.

Now, there might be another paradigm shift: our experiences at the heart of how AIs relate to emotion. This is my chance to participate in history in the making, like Mom did. My memories could be part of what makes an AI teacher receptive to a child's relentless inquisitiveness.

Still, there's this eeriness to the idea of my memories becoming no longer simply my own, an eeriness that pervades me with a disquiet I can't explain.

4. BEFORE EXPERIENCE BECOMES KNOWLEDGE

IN THE EVENING, I CALL MOM AND TELL HER THAT finally, officially, I'm becoming a memory donor.

"At last! Now society is guaranteed to benefit from your experiences too," she says, as though from outside the living room window, from the purple clouds above the skyline of concrete rectangles that always seems to undergird our phone conversations.

"Yeah, I'll be sharing that psychological wealth and maybe for the sake of technological progress. The archivist I met with asked if they can use my memories as a way for AIs to understand emotions."

"Oh, now it's robots in addition to people who get to benefit from our memories?" she asks, words tinged with delight.

"Sounds like it'll be robots that help people. AIs that will be teachers, coaches, and ambient assistants."

"What a way for your memories to be part of something beyond you. Mine are just slated to be studied for historical and anthropological purposes."

"You never know. If you signed an agreement that looks anything like the one they asked me to go over, the archive has your permission to use any donated memories for 'research projects' so long as they make efforts to maintain your anonymity."

"I'm sure that's in my donor agreement too, though I didn't make it through enough of that legalese to find out."

"I didn't make it very far with the legalese either. I ran it through a plain-language summary bot."

"And to think bots of the future should be able to read our moods as easily as they read contracts now. Who knows what they'll do next with our memories. Intelligent plants?"

"I can imagine that. The wise trees watching over the world centuries from now as the descendants of shrubs that learned from our lived experiences."

"Aw, what a lovely idea."

"Yeah, I'm sure that with time, there will only be more amazing uses for our memories."

"No doubt."

Then I'm out of preamble, and it's time to bring up what I've been meaning to during this phone call—what I've been meaning to during all the years of postponing officially enrolling myself as a donor. The moon rising over the distant mountains seems to be a sign that I can't put this off any longer.

"It's exciting and all, but does being a memory donor ever make you…self-conscious?" I ask, hoping the question won't start making her self-conscious. "Do you ever feel weird that something you're experiencing or remembering will have an existence beyond you?"

"Oh, I used to feel something like that, but I haven't for a long time."

"What changed?"

"Eventually, I got used to the idea that my memories will have their own existence. The same way I got used to simply having memories. I was self-conscious about that for years."

"About just having memories?" I ask, feeling like I misheard what Mom just said.

"Right. It's hard to explain. Especially because, looking back, that self-consciousness seems strange. But I'll try to describe it. When I was a teenager, I had this thought that if you consider your life so far, it's all just memories—past experiences your mind has held onto. So I became self-conscious about what I was experiencing, because I was concerned about what kinds of memories I'd end up with, what kind of life I'd end up with. That made thinking about the future a matter of figuring out what memories I'd be happy about as an adult."

"Wow, I've never thought about life and memories that way."

"Most people probably don't. For good reason. That perspective puts pressure on the present moment to be obviously positive or meaningful or productive. To be *something*. And sometimes it should be a certain something, but other times the present moment should just be whatever it is."

"So what got you to change your perspective on memories?"

"There wasn't any one thing. Eventually, I realized all we ever really have is the present moment, along with our thoughts and the actions we can take in that moment. We don't know what will ultimately come of the moment we're experiencing. All we can do is treat it as real—as significant—and do the best we can with it. That doesn't mean the future isn't important. Of course it is, but what we actually have to work with is our experience of being in successive moments. Whether they become memories we'll be happy with or researchers get insights from, that comes later. And whatever that is will have some meaning we can work with later."

"Then what you're saying is there's a difference between experience and memory. They're related but shouldn't influence each other unduly."

"Right, something like that. It's weird to think about this after not really thinking about it for so long. What I mainly took away from it all was that memories, or any kind of information, really, can become something more than a record of the events they came from. Memories carry moments forward to become something meaningful in different ways. What we have now in the present moment includes what remains of the present moments our past selves experienced—memories of those times and what they mean to us now."

Mom's words are perplexing, like poetry in a language that uses my native tongue with jarring idiosyncrasy. Then, in the silence that follows, my mind makes some tentative sense of things. Memory is information about a past state that endures in a way that could impact future states; the memory archive allows the past states of a person to inform present and future states of society—and soon AI companions.

5. INTUITION AND REASON

MOM'S WORDS REVERBERATE THROUGH EVERYTHING. Even here at work, the causal paths I chart all echo the truth of the human condition she pointed out, the holographic cartography gesturing at a larger truth beyond people—about the world: everything unfolds only moment by moment.

How had I missed that all this time? Well, it's not like I've been totally oblivious to the fact that consciousness only inhabits an ongoing now—that thin, relentlessly moving sliver in the continuum of time—but somehow it has always seemed like we have more than that. Which is true. We have all this stuff and all these possibilities in all the hours and days ahead, in the time I seem to have—seven more hours of daylight, ten more days until the end of the month. The next three hours are mine—to spend on work, sure, but to do that as I see fit with breaks and, if I want, chitchat with coworkers.

Mom's right, though: all we can ever do with stuff and possibilities and the time we have is through thought and action in the present moment, always within the limits of the human condition. We're only able to be in one place at any given time, seeing from a single vantage point, thinking one thought at a time. This quintessential reality must have been obscured by my intuitive sense of time's passage—like my intuitive sense of gravity, an unconscious comprehension of the order the world imposes and of the agency that order affords.

And doesn't sufficient agency within imposed order make us oblivious of that order's true nature? Within the limits of our singular existence in a singular moment, there is a richness of experience with enough agency to constitute meaningful freedom. Everything we've built in this world has been done through our existence across successive moments, our ability to use freedom within the limits of the moment to overcome those limits, to join one moment to the next and the next. What we can do in a second is the basis of what we can do in an hour, in a day, in a year. Our reach extends beyond the moment because we know how to use our thoughts and actions in the moment to that end.

The nascent causal map glowing in front of me is evidence of that. As it roughly traces the rise and fall of a long-defunct neurotech company, the chart shows how this now obscure venture unfurled its corporate reach step by incremental step. Everything that comprises the chart—like everything that comprises our lives—is causes and effects, someone using a moment for the sake of causing an effect on a later moment, whether the very next one or one that's far off. A stark reminder that while all animals harness causality, we have become uncontested masters of it through our unparalleled cognitive capacities and the technologies they have made possible.

6. ON THE CONDITION OF TOGETHERNESS

OF COURSE, I'M STILL THINKING ABOUT ALL THIS when I'm back on the sofa in the memory archive's relaxing waiting room. How could I not think about it here?

And it might be only here that I can come to the conclusion I now arrive at: Yes, all we ever truly have is the present moment, along with our thoughts and actions in it, but future generations, whether of humans or AIs, could have more than we do— if nothing else, through our contributions to their thoughts and the possibilities those make available. That's what memory donation is for, and what has always been integral to the enterprise of human progress.

Dr. Burndle comes in several minutes after I've gotten comfortable with the idea that we can't extend the present moment, but we can expand what's possible in it—as if I've been afforded enough time to reach and linger in this perspective.

Once I'm in the consultation room and again sitting across the desk from her, I tell Dr. Burndle, "I've thought about it, and I'd like my memories to be part of the Synthetic Empathy project, but only if my mother's memories are also used whenever mine are."

Dr. Burndle's eyes widen. A split second later, she smiles as though pleased that I've passed a test I didn't know I was taking—or met an expectation that's been kept secret from me.

"It should be no problem to make the necessary arrangements," she says.

And a relief I never could have expected ripples through me. It seems to dissolve several pounds' worth of some anxiety I had no idea I was carrying. I know this sensation of sudden lightness will stay with me in my memories, and inexplicably I also know that it will be of significance to someone in the future.

THE COST OF LIVING - BY REBECCA BURTON

I STARED OUT OF THE CLASSROOM WINDOW AT THE
RAIN. ACROSS THE STREET, THE SCHOOL IN BLOCK J
WAS ON THE SAME LEVEL AS US, AND I WONDERED IF
the kids over there were as bored as I was. Or maybe
their Administrator was nicer and hadn't scheduled
calculus for a Friday afternoon.

In the distance, the giant outlines of Farming
Mechs were just visible over the city walls, silhouetted
against the setting sun. Their many-armed bodies
moved ponderously over the fields as they harvested
the food that fed the City.

A blare of trumpets snapped my attention back
to the front of the room. On the holoscreen, the

familiar logo of the Ministry of Works glowed blue and gold—a silhouette of a man and a woman, flanked by a Farm Mech and a Construction Mech, with the motto "Building a Better World" scrolling underneath.

A familiar mixture of awe and revulsion roiled in my stomach. The Ministry symbolised everything I longed for and everything I feared the most.

It was the same PSA they played at the end of every week, reminding us all what we owed to the Ministry—food, clothes, roofs over our heads, and electricity to run our City—and what they expected of us in turn: the service of those few with the ability to pilot the Mechs. We'd seen the same video hundreds, if not thousands, of times. Most of the other kids had already spun around to chat with each other or send messages on their handscreens under the desks. But I couldn't tear my eyes away.

I knew I would be able to pilot a Mech. And, if I volunteered, the Ministry could give me the one thing I craved more than anything. But I would lose everything else.

The bright colors of the propaganda video finally faded out, and our maths teacher made his escape, followed by most of the class. Everyone had somewhere better to be on a Friday night, even if only a few of us could legally drink.

A bright flash of color appeared in my peripheral vision, and then my best friend, Missy, was perching her butt on the edge of my desk.

"Earth to Ari. Are you there, Ari?" She waved a hand in front of my eyes, and I swatted weakly at it.

"Sod off, Mis," I replied. "I thought you had to hurry to work tonight?"

"Nope." She waved her screen under my nose too fast for me to read any of the words on the display. "I got fired by email. Isn't it great?"

"Um, if you say so…"

"Of course it's great," Missy said firmly. "It means more time for shopping! You gotta come with me. It's going to be fun."

"Yay…shopping…With what money, Mis? You just lost your job." As I spoke, I tucked my hair more securely under my hood and pulled my oversized sweater sleeves down over my hands. If we were going out in public, I needed my armor to protect me.

Missy frowned at my movements. "You know, you're quite pretty, really. If you ever let anyone actually see you, you'd definitely have a boyfriend. Or a girlfriend. Just like that." She snapped her fingers.

"I don't want one," I muttered. "Either one."

"Fine, you don't have to date if you don't want to," she replied, sighing. Probably thinking about her latest breakup. Missy went through dates faster than I used up my handscreen data. "But you could at least let me find you some pretty clothes. Maybe some makeup. You'd look great in a dress, I promise. There's no need to hide your body from everyone all the time."

"I'm not hiding it from other people!" I blurted the words out before I could stop myself.

Missy's eyes went wide, and she clapped a hand across my mouth. "Don't say that," she hissed as we both scanned the room for anyone who might have overheard us.

Thankfully, all the other kids had already left the classroom, but that didn't mean we were completely unobserved. Nowhere in the City was free of cameras. I could only hope no one was paying attention to this particular classroom, in just another identical block in the Battery Cages.

I peeled Missy's hand off my face. "It's okay, Mis," I said. "They're not coming."

"But they might have done!" Unshed tears welled at the corners of her eyes. "You need to be more careful. I don't know what I'd do if they took you away."

I huffed a breath at her, trying to hide my own emotions. "I'm not going anywhere." Neither of us believed me.

"I'm sorry," Missy said, grabbing my hand between hers and squeezing. "I shouldn't have pushed. I already knew…well, I guessed. I should have just left it. If they come for you, it will be all my fault."

I squeezed back, her hands cold in mine. "I should have told you already, but I was scared. Ma needs me. Rami needs me. I can't let anyone find out yet."

Scared: yes, that was one word for what I was. But a small part of me longed to be discovered. It was my ticket out of this dump and my one chance at becoming who I should have been. But I couldn't abandon my family. And I couldn't leave Missy.

A FEW HOURS LATER, MISSY HAD FINALLY FINISHED her shopping, and I could escape. The small mall in the base of our Block hadn't been good enough for her, so she'd dragged me all the way over to the big mall in Block C. And then she'd deserted me there.

Well, to be fair, I'd deserted her at the mention of the party she was going to in Block H. Parties weren't exactly my favourite activity; somewhere below scrubbing toilets and above the annual Block Festival on my personal list of hell.

The S-train was almost empty on the journey back, and I slumped in my seat, avoiding eye contact with the few other passengers. Above our heads, a series of identical holographic posters from the Ministry of Works shouted their identical hyperbolic messages down at us.

> *Do you feel like you don't belong?*
> *Is your body not your own? Then*
> *come to the Ministry of Works for*

> *testing! You could be a Mech Pilot—*
> *the saviors of our city!—and receive*
> *free medical care to live the life you*
> *were born to live!!*

I did my best not to look. Who knew if they were monitoring for people who spent just a little too long looking at the posters in their endless quest for new Pilots?

Everyone knew someone who had been taken away for testing. Only those whose dysphoria in their own bodies was severe enough could cope with the feeling of wrongness that came with linking to a Mech. That was who the Ministry searched for so relentlessly. Its precious Pilots.

Occasionally, someone failed the tests and came back again—closemouthed and tired. But mostly they never came back at all.

The train arrived at the Block G station, and I hurried onto the platform and away from the posters' demands.

Our flat was on the fiftieth floor, which meant a long ride in the lifts from the subterranean S-train station but also meant we were above the smog. The windows faced east, and in the morning sunlight would flood into the tiny living area, warming the whole flat. From the windows, you could see all the way across the wall to where the Farm Mechs roamed and, even farther, to the mountains beyond, where tiny specks of flying Mechs serviced and repaired the hydroelectric plants that powered the City.

The only good thing about going home was the view.

"Ma, I'm home," I called as I unlocked the front door.

"Welcome back, love." The faint voice drifted to me from the largest bedroom—still barely big enough for a double bed and a chest of drawers and space to squeeze out of the door between them—and I followed it to find my mother sitting up in bed and smiling at me.

She looked tired and drawn, as usual. The accident that had left her leg shattered into twenty pieces had also gifted her the joys of chronic pain and early-onset arthritis, and there was only so much the doctors could do.

"I had a letter from my surgeon today," Ma said as I sat down on the edge of her bed. "There's this new treatment they can try that might give me a bit more mobility. And they reckon it might reduce my pain levels, too."

"That's great, Ma," I said, but my heart sank in my chest. "How much does it cost?"

Basic health care was free in the City, along with a room of your own and food and clothing. No one was homeless or hungry or naked. But only the most basic things were free. If you wanted something more interesting than nutrient gruel to eat, you had to pay.

If you wanted to look fashionable—or at least not stick out as dirt poor in mass-issued clothing—you had to pay. The same applied to medical care.

Ma's face fell. "Not much," she mumbled. "Only twenty thousand."

I tried to stifle my gasp and failed. After the accident, when Ma couldn't work anymore, she was entitled to a pension from the government, as well as disability benefits. But together they only totaled ten thousand a year, and our savings had already been wiped out.

Ma and I were still wearing clothes we bought before the accident, fraying as they were, and had both resigned ourselves to living off free gruel, but Rami needed proper food and clothes. I couldn't send him to school in free-issue—that would basically be admitting we were broke and asking his classmates to look down on him—but I wished he wouldn't outgrow his clothes so fast.

And he was smart—so freaking smart; he might even make it into the Tech Schools next year. Which meant a real chance for him to have a future, but also meant serious school fees to pay. I'd already started scrimping and saving what I could to meet the entrance fees, and I had nowhere near enough.

And now Ma's doctor wanted another twenty thousand...

"I'll see what I can do," I said, forcing a smile. "Is Rami home yet?"

Ma knew that I was avoiding talking about money, but she let me change the subject. "No, I think he has his extra programming class tonight."

"Oh, right." How could I have forgotten that? Another thing I had somehow managed to pay for out of our meager budget. "I'm gonna go do my homework, then. Anything you need, Ma?"

Ma patted my hand. "No, love. I'm fine. You go study." She must have been so bored stuck in that tiny room all day, but she could still smile for me.

I threw my arms around her and dragged her into a hug. "I love you, Ma," I whispered, and then dashed from the room before she could see the tears in my eyes. I wanted so badly to make everything go back to how it had been before, when we were all happy and our biggest worry was what film to pick for family movie night, but there was nothing I could do.

Safely hidden in my own room, I flopped down on the bed. I should study or eat, but I couldn't face the thought. Rami was the bright one, not me—studying wouldn't help—and food would only curdle in my stomach.

And I couldn't face the thought of showering. The cold reflection of the bathroom mirror only highlighted everything that was wrong with me, and there was nowhere to hide. At least when I was dressed I could disguise the parts of myself I hated the most and avoid seeing the rest. Naked, I had no way to avoid reality.

I couldn't protect my family, and I couldn't fix myself.

All I could do was bury my head under my pillow and hope that sleep would come quickly. At least if I was unconscious, existing wouldn't hurt quite so fucking much.

THE NEXT MORNING, I WOKE EARLY AND SNUCK OUT of the flat. I needed to think, and I needed to escape from Ma and Rami's hopeful eyes. There had to be some way I could make the money we needed.

The lift ride to the base of the Block took forever, but luckily it was a Saturday, so not many people were around. When we finally reached the ground, I hurried out of the Block's main doors to the park across the street.

In this part of the Battery Cages, the Blocks were arranged in a hexagonal pattern, with a public park in the center of each cell. It was meant to keep us all healthy, give us a chance to get outside and exercise in the sunshine—or some such shit—but most of the parks turned into places for kids to hang out and drink and smoke when they were too young to get into the Block bars.

But at 6 a.m. on a damp October day, even the most hardcore were home, safe in bed.

I found a bench that was protected from the drizzle by a scrawny tree and slumped down onto the damp wooden seat.

Ma's surgery—that was the main problem. Rami's school fees were a smaller issue. They wouldn't be due for at least another year, and we could get loans to pay them up front. Ma's pension would be enough to pay the interest and chip away at the capital—especially if we both lived off the basic citizen entitlements—and when Rami graduated and got a good job, it would all be worth it.

But where was I going to find twenty thousand? Whatever small part-time jobs I could get to fit around school would pay a tiny fraction of that. I would have to work for years…

I would do anything for Ma, but the thought of years of crappy jobs, trapped in this body that didn't belong to me, made me want to start running and never stop. Ever since puberty, the feeling of wrongness had grown stronger until I could barely stand it. I could hardly think about tomorrow, never mind years or decades of living like this.

My only option for relief was the Ministry.

And if I went there, I would never see Ma or Rami or Missy ever again.

I lay down on the bench and stared at the bare branches of the tree and the gray sky above. If anyone saw me, I could pretend that the moisture on my face was from the rain, and it wouldn't be a total lie.

The Ministry had power and money. Without their Pilots, the City wouldn't exist. If anyone could arrange Ma's surgery or get Rami into a good school, it would be them. Would that be worth the price? Or was that just me putting myself ahead of my family?

And how could I tell the difference?

A flicker of movement, the bright flash of metal moving across the gray sky, caught my eye, and I started upright to get a better look. Mechs and Pilots were forbidden from entering the City, but food and goods had to be delivered somehow, so it wasn't unusual to see freight Mechs moving overhead as they ferried cargo to the designated storage zones in each sector.

This one must have been on its way back: the massive cargo container that made up the bulk of its body was missing, leaving only the small Pilot capsule with its network of scaffolding for attaching to the containers. And it was moving wrong.

I shaded my eyes with one hand as I peered up at the jittering Mech. It seemed to shudder from side to side as it flew and ... it was falling! Jumping up from the bench, I scuttled backward, away from the Mech that was growing ever larger as it plummeted toward the park. Toward me.

There was no time to run—there wasn't even time to think. I darted behind a tree and crouched down, arms over my head like that had any hope of protecting me from several tons of metal falling from the sky.

I'd barely curled into myself when the world exploded around me.

All I could do was hold on until soil and debris finished raining down, and then, somehow, I was still alive. A trickle of warmth ran down the side of my face. When I put my hand to my head, it came away red with blood. But I was alive.

I leaned out from behind my tree and gasped at the devastation that had taken place. The Mech had shattered on impact, shedding enormous metal struts and sheets of fiberglass across the park. The bench I had been sitting on only a minute before had been split in two.

My hands started shaking. If I'd been any slower, if I hadn't noticed something wasn't right, that would have been me.

Clambering to my feet, I staggered toward home, giving a wide berth to the battered Pilot capsule, which had detached from the rest of the Mech and now lay upside down in the middle of what used to be a flowerbed. In the distance, I could hear sirens. Someone would be here soon to help the poor Pilot. And I would be long gone when they arrived.

Or, at least, that was my intention. Until I heard the voice calling for help.

"Is anyone there?" a voice called from the wreckage. Then there was a series of clanks. "Damn it. I think I'm stuck."

"Don't do it," I whispered to myself, but I was already limping across the crushed flowers to the side of the downed Mech. Bending down, I peered into the mess of metal and wires and shattered glass that was all that remained of the Pilot capsule. "Hello? Are you all right?"

"I've been better!" the Pilot called back cheerfully. "But I'm still kicking. Well, I would be if I could move my damn legs."

The sound of their voice gave my gaze a direction, and I finally found their shape among the debris. The Pilot hung upside down in their seat, held in by safety straps and the wires that ran from the chair into the back of their head. Tears in their jumpsuit and skin exposed flashes of bright metal rather than flesh, except for one cut on their temple that slowly seeped blood.

"I heard sirens," I replied as I wriggled a bit closer. I knew I shouldn't, but I couldn't help myself. "They'll be here soon to get you out."

Reaching behind themself with one hand, the Pilot pulled out the wires connecting them to the ship, then twisted their neck to look at me. They had pale gray eyes that seemed to glow in the gloom, and it felt like they could see right through me.

"Oh, you're hurt too," they said. "Sorry, this was the only open space I could get to once the engine started playing up. I hoped it would be empty this early."

I started reaching to touch the cut on my head and stopped myself, hiding my hands back in my sleeves. "I'm fine."

The Pilot narrowed their eyes as their gaze ran over me. "You're one of us, aren't you?" They must have seen me tense, because they hurried on. "Don't worry, I won't tell anyone. I'm Rhea. She/her." She stretched out a hand for me to shake.

Awkwardly, I reached toward her, kinking my elbow past a chunk of rock that might once have been a decorative statue until the Mech landed on it. Her fingers squeezed mine gently, cold where the crash had stripped the skin off the metal underneath. "I'm, er, Ari. Um…" All I could hear was the deafening silence of me not saying my own pronouns. I hurried on, saying the first thing that popped into my mind. "I've never met a Pilot before."

"Not many people have," Rhea replied, a sad smile tugging at one corner of her mouth. "It's good to meet you, Ari."

Voices behind me caught my attention, and I glanced over my shoulder. "They're here," I said to Rhea. "You'll be out soon." I offered her a smile, then wriggled free from the wreckage, her gray eyes watching me the whole way.

The paramedics quickly took my place, and I backed off, mingling with the crowd that had gathered at the edge of the park. Pulling my hood up to hide the cut on my head, I made myself invisible, but I didn't leave. I needed to know that Rhea made it out okay first.

Around me, the onlookers muttered about the dangers of Mechs and swapped stories of their cousin's friend who'd met a Pilot once, but it was all just gossip. I'd heard it before. None of it was real. But Rhea was.

It took a long time to cut her out, but at last she was lifted free and laid on a stretcher. As they wheeled her away, I saw her scanning the crowd, looking for someone. I stepped forward so she could see me, and a smile spread across her face.

As they were loading her into the ambulance, I realized this was my only chance to ask the question that had lived in my heart for so long. Dashing forward, I called out to her. "Was it worth it?"

My words could have meant anything, but she seemed to understand. She craned her neck to see me as the ambulance doors closed, her mouth quirking at the corners, and said a single word.

"Sometimes."

And then she was gone.

I slipped free of the crowd, which seemed settled in to watch the cleanup, and walked slowly back to our Block. I had come out this morning looking for answers and had only found more questions. But deep in my heart, where I didn't have to look at or acknowledge it yet, I had already made my decision.

FINDING THE MINISTRY OF WORKS WAS EASY. THEY had an office in each sector of the City where you could go to make a request for materials or pay an invoice. Or offer yourself for Pilot testing.

In our sector, the office was in Block C's shopping mall, sandwiched between a clothing store and a small kiosk selling sim games. The shop front was plain, the only sign it was even occupied a small plaque by the door with the Ministry's name and a three-word motto written underneath.

Serve to Live.

I curled my lip as I stared at the plaque. Obviously written by committee, it didn't mean anything. Or perhaps it meant too much. Flipping a rude gesture at the motto, I opened the door and stepped inside.

What I saw was disappointingly mundane. There was an ordinary reception desk, with an ordinary workscreen and an ordinary receptionist, and two other doors—one to either side of the desk. The receptionist glanced up as he heard the front door close behind me and smiled.

"Welcome to the Ministry of Works," he said. "How can I help you?"

I stumbled forward to stand in front of the counter. "I … er … I'm here to volunteer for the testing." The words came out in a rush, but it didn't seem to faze the receptionist. He'd probably seen plenty of people like me come through here.

"Name?" he asked.

"Ari."

"Pronouns?"

"They/them." As I said the words, a shudder ran through me. I'd finally said out loud what I'd always felt and always had to hide… My eyes grew damp, and I hurriedly scrubbed at them with my sleeve before the receptionist could look back up from his screen.

It seemed to take him a very long time to enter those simple details, but when he looked up again, his face was kind. "ID, please."

I handed my card over and waited, my hands gripping each other tightly until he finished with the ID and handed it back. Standing, he picked up a folder from the desk and motioned me to follow him through the door to the left of the reception desk.

As he opened the door, I gestured back at the desk and the front door. "What about…?"

"Don't worry about it. One of my colleagues will take over." He pushed the door fully open and waved me inside. "Please, take a seat so we can have a proper conversation."

I stepped into the small room. The walls and floor and ceiling were all painted white. In the middle of the room, there was a small table, on which sat a jug of water and two glasses, and two chairs waited for occupants. The only other feature of the room was a second door on the opposite wall from where we entered.

The receptionist ushered me to a chair, then sat down across from me and began to pour water for both of us.

With nothing else to look at, I studied his face. He was an older man, with kind, smiling eyes. Paternal, or avuncular, perhaps; I didn't know. I couldn't remember my father and had never had an uncle. But everything about him seemed to make him look trustworthy. I wondered if the Ministry had recruited him for this role because of that or if they had made him that way.

The click of a folder opening dragged me back from my thoughts. The folder now lay in front of me, revealing what appeared to be a contract. The receptionist leaned over and placed a pen in front of me.

"This is our standard Pilot contract," he said. "Please read it carefully and sign if you are happy with the terms."

I glanced at the paper, but the words swam before my eyes. It was impossible to read. And it didn't matter—as long as they could do what I asked.

Ignoring the contract, I looked up at the receptionist instead. "I have a condition," I said.

"A condition?" he asked. "Medical, or ... ?"

"Not like that. A ... requirement. If I pass the testing, there's something you—the Ministry—has to do for me."

He didn't seem surprised. "And what is that condition?"

"If I pass," I said, "you have to promise that my Ma will get the medical care she needs. And someone needs to take care of Rami. He's too smart not to get a proper education."

"Ah, your brother?" the receptionist asked. "Yes, of course. No problem."

I couldn't believe it. This was too easy. "Really? No problem?"

The receptionist nodded and pointed to the contract. "Clause 3.5 – *any expenses authorised by the Pilot Candidate on behalf of their family or friends will be met by the Ministry and added to the Pilot Candidate's debt to be discharged via their usual salary deductions,*" he read.

"Salary? I thought …"

The receptionist snorted. "Of course there's a salary. This is a job. You really should read the full contract." He paused until it became obvious that I couldn't or wouldn't follow his suggestion.

"All right," he continued, "as a fully qualified Pilot, you will receive a salary, from which will be deducted costs of accommodation and food and ongoing medical care. You can also authorize costs to be deducted on behalf of your family or for a portion to be set aside for discretionary spending."

He must have seen my confusion from my face. "Clothes, makeup, entertainment media—these kinds of things. All the basics are covered by the living expense deductions, but many of our Pilots like to choose a few extra luxuries."

"Oh," I said, still trying to process everything he was saying. "And debt?"

"Ah, yes. There are two elements to the debt all Pilots have. First, there is the initial medical costs for the operations necessary to allow you to interface with a Mech. At the same time, this allows us to sculpt your body to meet your requirements. The changes we make will also allow further, simpler adaptations later. Many of our Pilots choose to increase their debts to purchase additional body-forms or alternatives."

I blinked at him. "Body-forms?" Apparently sentences of more than three syllables were beyond me, but he understood.

"The basic mods we give you can be adapted. So, for example, some of our Pilots have fluid genders. They are female one day and male another, and neutral on yet another. By purchasing additional body-forms, they can make these changes as easily as you or I change our clothes."

I nodded dumbly.

"Now, the second part of the debt is the training fees for the Pilot program. Just the same as student loans. Nice and straightforward." The receptionist—no, the recruiter—paused. "Any questions?"

"What happens if I pay off my debt?" I asked. "Can I go home?"

For the first time, he looked uncomfortable. "I ... well ... usually our Pilots choose to make additional purchases, and—"

I cut him off. "But what if I don't do that, and I do pay off my debt? What happens?"

"I ... I don't know." The recruiter shook his head. "I don't think it's ever happened before."

I nodded. This was more like what I expected, rather than talk of salaries and benefits and discretionary spending. No one had ever come back from the Ministry, and now I knew why.

Another thought crossed my mind. "Why are you telling me all this? I haven't tested yet. What if I don't pass?"

The recruiter laughed. "You would have never gotten this far if we weren't already sure. We already know everything about you, Ari. You passed the second you walked through the front door."

A cold shiver ran down my spine. I had thought I had been careful, that no one knew—except maybe Missy—but I had been wrong. If I hadn't walked in voluntarily, how long would it have taken before the Ministry came for me?

"But I haven't signed yet," I said. "I could still walk away." I wanted my words to come out brave and strong and fearless, but I could hear the tremor in my own voice.

The recruiter raised an eyebrow. "Are you really not going to sign?" he asked, voice tinged with laughter. "I think we know you better than you know yourself."

I chewed on my lower lip. Was he right? Did they know enough about me to predict everything I would do?

But then, hadn't I already made my decision before I even arrived?

I glanced down at the contract again, and at the notes he had made alongside about my wishes. The Ministry could take care of Ma and Rami easily. The surgery would be nothing to them, and Rami's school fees would barely register. They'd probably even be pleased to add them to my "debt" and have me further under their control. If I could use this opportunity to protect my family, wouldn't it be worth it?

Selfless? I snorted at myself. Is that what I was pretending to be? Naturally, I was only doing this for my family; never mind that if I signed this contract, I might never see them again. Never mind that I had walked in here, at least in part, for my own selfish reasons, because I longed to feel at peace in my own body. But this was the only way I could see to fix things, for Ma and Rami, and for myself. That's why I chose to come here in the first place.

I thought of the injured Pilot lying in the dust and the dirt, half crushed under the weight of her own

Mech. I thought of her gray eyes that looked right through me, and the feel of her cold metal fingers clasped in mine. I thought of the wry smile that pulled at her face as she offered me a single honest word: *Sometimes.*

I picked up the pen.

"Where do I sign?"

A STORY OF CIRCLE AND BREATH - BY MEGAN WILDHOOD

A child's mother died. She was nine until she heard the news. Then, she forgot some years and that she even had a younger sister. She became little again, the only motherless child.

Just before she became the only motherless child, she watched the mother lay in bed, thinking it was a normal day. The mother had laid in bed a lot, especially lately. The mother's eyes and mouth were wide, like she'd wanted to see an angel for a long time, and finally one had appeared.

The child grabbed the mother's hand. "I want it to be my turn to tell the bedtime story."

The mother attempted to squeeze the child's hand.

"Okay," said the child after a long silence. "There was once a lot of time. There was so much time that it was hard to move through all of it, but people were never late because there was so much time everywhere. It was slippery but also wrinkly, so you had to learn how to slide around on it. Everybody fell down a lot, but it was soft, so it didn't hurt. Mostly, it was just fun to skate around on, and if you fell down, you did not have to get up right away, because time would fold in over you for a little while, like it was protecting you. People kept trying to move really fast like they always had for a while, but then they got tired. They sat down and looked up at the sky more. They saw flowers they did not think were there before. They saw people they had always passed and started to remember them. There was so much time to get through that they started to think there always would be time, so they stopped going places.

"But then someone figured out how to trap time in big black bags. She was also really big, but she was also invisible. She was also really strong, so she could carry lots of time all at once, and nobody knew where she went with it. Some people started to have less time than other people, and nobody could figure out why. The people who had less time had to start moving faster, and they had to start choosing whether they would help someone who fell down or if they would keep going just so they wouldn't be late. People started to forget how to help each other because the big, strong, invisible girl was getting away with taking so much time.

"But the girl was not keeping the time for herself like everyone thought she was. She was sneaking into hospitals and pouring it all over the sickest kids she could find. The doctors did not understand how so many kids could be magically better, and some of them started to worry that they wouldn't have jobs if this kept happening. They talked about how they could stop this from happening, but they didn't know why their patients were getting better, so their patients kept getting better.

"One man who could see everything finally saw the girl. He was a very sad man, and a lot of people thought that he was sad because he could see everything, but it was really the other way around. He went to one of the places that was slower and harder to move through and waited for the girl to come for a lot of time. When she came, he said hello to her, which scared her, since she wasn't used to anyone ever seeing her. 'How much time is there left?' he asked.

"'I don't know exactly,' the girl said. 'But it's harder and harder to find.' The man stepped closer to the girl and asked, 'Enough for the rest of the kids in the hospitals?' The girl started to look as sad as the man did and shook her head. The man held out his arms to her. 'Then take the rest of mine.' The girl looked up at the man and then toward the hospitals and then back at the man. She did not know what to do."

"Mommy, what should she do?"

‹ TENTEN › - BY PERCY EID

STARS. NIGHT.

Stars. The sound of soothing waves crashing against the shores of a beach can be heard. In the distance, the ocean merges with the starry night sky, and a mote of light blinks in and out amid the celestials.

.. ... / - .... . .-. . / .-.. --- ...- . / --- ..- - / - .... .
.-. . . ..--..

(Is there love out there?)

HOSPITAL. NIGHT.

In the dark, little beads of light from various machineries and medical equipment can be seen. A steady beeping punctuates the silence, accompanied by someone's tender breathing, and, backlit by the lights of a faraway apartment building twinkling through the hospital window, a blanketed figure is laid on the bed.

Someone turns on the light.

White walls and white sheets. The sound of a clock, ticking, can be heard. Sitting beside the bed, Maria had dozed off from fatigue while still holding the hand of her sleeping son, Tenten, whose small frame barely uses up half of the bed space.

A nurse enters the room and smiles politely at Maria. Rubbing the sleep from her tired eyes and wiping at her crusted tears with the blue shawl wrapped around her neck, Maria halfheartedly smiles back.

Deep in slumber, Tenten's rhythmic breathing fogs the plastic mask of the ventilator covering his mouth. Translucent tubes coil around his arms, connecting him to a life support machine and an IV bag. By his bedside, the cardiac monitor beeps every few seconds. Maria wearily glances at her son—eyes heavy with rain, though not yet ready to burst.

After a while, she goes out into the hallway and stops in front of a vending machine. She puts a few coins in; one falls to the floor and rolls a few feet. Maria walks over to it and picks it up, groaning, her bones not as young as they used to be. She inserts the coin in the slot, and the machine hums, the coils quietly whirring inside as a bottle of juice shifts forward from the top row behind the glass. It falls and clatters against the dense metal and plastic at the bottom. Maria takes the bottle from the depository and uncaps it.

Maria returns to sit by Tenten's bedside. She looks at him for a moment, wistful. Then she inches closer and taps her index finger lightly on his arm.

-.-. --- -- . / .... --- -- .

(Come home)

Someone raps lightly on the door. Another nurse lets himself in. Maria looks up at him, and the nurse smiles and nods. She checks the clock on the wall: 8:55 p.m. She squeezes Tenten's hand for a fleeting second before slowly getting up to leave.

LAUNDROMAT. NIGHT.

Somewhere in the quiet alleys of the city, a laundromat spumes steam from its vents and fluorescent lights through its windows. MARIA'S WASH. Inside, a young lady in a baggy polycotton uniform is sitting by the glass doors. She's stacking bars of soap and sachets of laundry detergent in a hamper. The door swings open, hitting the small bell above the frame as Maria walks inside. She's cheerfully greeted by her assistant, but Maria just shakes her head sullenly. Understanding, her assistant nods solemnly and goes back to her station to resume her work.

Deeper inside the shop, a handful of people are waiting by the rows of washing machines lining the walls, some vibrating, emitting a low and steady hum. Peering through the door of his washer, a man in an oversized sweater with a cup of coffee in his hand sways, hypnotized by the swirling colors of soap, water, and laundry inside the appliance. The detergent-infused water seems to mimic a raging sea during a storm.

A young lady wearing a burka is seated at the center of the room on a white bench. She's reading a magazine, *The Divine Feminine,* and from its cover glares a woman with a third eye. Flipping through the pages, the young lady scans various headlines: 10 TIPS ON HOW TO USE YOUR SACRAL CHAKRA, HOW TO MEET YOUR ALIEN FAMILY, and ARE YOU PLEIADIAN OR DRACONIC?

There's also a mohawked man covered in tattoos, headbanging to classical music on his headphones while rummaging inside a sack of clothes. Beside him is an old lady with beady eyes and a white wool of hair, innocently listening to heavy metal music blasting from her earphones. And at the far corner of the room is a person in a bear mascot suit, watching sadly as a panda mascot suit whirls inside a washer.

The door swings open, and the bell dings again. This time, an old man sporting aviator goggles enters, dragging a massive sheet of thick cloth through the door. Maria and her assistant stare in awe and dismay at such an abundance of fabric. But the man just proudly beams at them, his teeth twinkling in a grin. Maria's assistant begrudgingly takes the unknowable sort of material and, determined to get it all inside, proceeds to stuff it into their biggest machine but fails miserably.

Maria sighs, walks to the far end of the room, and takes a seat behind the counter. She fishes a pair of glasses from behind the desk, puts them on before pulling up a large notebook, and starts scribbling.

Well into the night, all the lights in the laundromat are switched off apart from the lamp on Maria's desk. All alone, Maria is still writing in the notebook, squinting under the dim lamp. Every so often, she takes a tag of paper from a plastic box on the floor, looks at it, and returns to her scribbling. After a while, her assistant walks out from the staff room carrying a bag and wearing casual clothes. She waves goodbye to Maria, who looks up and smiles. On her way out, she flips the door sign: CLOSED.

FLASHBACK. BEACH. NIGHT.

Maria is in her twenties. She's at the coast by the city. Her blue shawl is fluttering in the wind, and a leather-strap bag is hanging from her shoulder. She is pulling a wooden boat, lurching it across the sand. The only sounds that can be heard are the waves lapping at the shore and her occasional grunting. Soon the waves reach the hull of the boat, gently lifting it toward the sea. Maria quickly hops inside. She then picks up the oars and starts to paddle forward.

A few moments pass, and Maria is still paddling, the waves beneath her gently swaying the boat. She stands up, steadying herself against the boat's gunwale as she stares into the distance, grasping her shawl as it billows in the wind. All around her is just darkness, and the city lights by the coast are shrinking farther and farther away. Maria unzips her bag and takes out a flashlight and a handheld radio. She points the flashlight to the stars and sends a message in Morse code.

.- ..-. . / -.-- --- ..- / --- ..- - / - .... . .-. . ..-..

(Are you out there?)

She waits for a response.

.- ..-. . / -.-- --- ..- / ... - .. .-.. .-.. / .- .-.. .. ... - . ..-..

(Are you still alive?)

A moment passes.

.-- .- .. - .. -. --. / ..-. --- .-. / -.-- --- ..-

(Waiting for you)

Maria sits down on the boat, still holding up her light.

Percy Eid

-.. .- -.. / -.-. --- -- ./ .... --- -- .
(Dad come home)

-.-. --- -- . / .... --- -- .
(Come home)

-.-. --- -- . / .... --- -- .
(Come home)

Maria lies down on the wooden sole of her vessel. Despite the ache in her arms from being held up for so long, she continues flickering her light to the starry night. Around her, the dark sea stretches out endlessly. Eventually, Maria struggles to keep her eyes open as sleep begins to overcome her, until finally she gives in and closes her eyes. Suddenly, her radio crackles to life, followed by a muffled beeping that seems like a pattern. Behind her closed eyes, the darkness glows red as if a bright light is shining through her thin eyelids. It blinks in sequence:

.. / .- -- / .... . .-. .
(I am here)

LAUNDROMAT. NIGHT.

Maria has fallen asleep at her desk in the laundromat; her faint snoring ruffles the pages of the notebook beneath her cheek. Just out of reach of her fingertips, perched on the desk's surface, is a framed photograph of a little girl beside a seaman. And wrapped around the sailor's broad shoulders is a blue shawl.

Beside her face, her phone is vibrating. A small button of light from the phone is flickering on and off with the beeps, illuminating Maria's face in steady staccato. Maria stirs and wakes. She sits up, rubbing her eyes, sees the beeping phone, and picks it up. Maria gazes at the pale light of the screen as she reads the message, and her eyes widen in fear.

HOSPITAL. NIGHT.

Maria is in the hospital hallway, rushing to the room where her son is, but she's intercepted by the doctor just as she's about to enter. The doctor looks apologetic. Maria peeks her head in the room and sees Tenten sleeping soundly. He's breathing, but his heart monitor is beeping more rapidly than before.

The doctor delivers news to Maria in the hallway, and she sighs in relief. She smiles and nods but remains worried. Inside the room, Tenten is breathing more steadily now, and the heart monitor is back to its slow beeps. The doctor sighs and shakes his head. Maria just nods as the doctor goes on his way. Tentatively, she approaches her son and sits beside

Percy Eid

him on the bed. She lightly brushes his hair. After a moment, she taps on his forehead.

-... . / --- -.- .- -.--
(Be okay)

-.-. --- -- . / .... --- -- .
(Come home)

.-.. --- ...- . / -.-- --- ..-
(Love you)

Eventually, Maria is recalled by the nurses. She takes a moment to plant a tender kiss on Tenten's forehead before heading back out again—turning the lights off in the room as she walks out the door. A few moments after she leaves, the heart monitor beeps.

.. / .- -- / .... . .-. .
(I am here)

MARIA'S HOUSE. DAY.

Maria's alarm goes off, beeping incessantly. Shrugging off her blanket, she wakes, sits up in bed, and turns off her alarm. Maria goes to check the fridge for breakfast, takes out a bottle of milk, and pours it in a glass. Leaning on the kitchen counter, she drinks the milk slowly. She glances down and sees the mound of dirty dishes in the sink. Maria sighs, knowing she can't neglect doing the household chores forever.

After cleaning the living room for the first time in a while, she makes her way to Tenten's bedroom. Sweeping the vacuum across the stale floor, she lifts up Tenten's blue hanging blanket adorned with yellow stars and sticks the vacuum underneath the bed. Something catches on the suction, and Maria pulls the vacuum back, revealing a dusty toy spaceship stuck on the brush. She smiles tenderly at it before placing it in a cardboard box along with Tenten's other toys.

Later in the day, Maria finishes hanging the bedsheets on the clotheslines over the balcony. The sun hangs low in the sky, and Maria finally washes the dishes while a song plays on the radio. Suds of dishwashing soap gather around her wrists, and, for a moment, Maria contemplates her reflection in the foamy water. Suddenly, the melody from the radio is interrupted by static, followed by silence and syncopated beeping.

-- .- -- .-

(Mama)

Maria stops.

-- .- -- .-

(Mama)

She looks up from the sink and rushes to the radio—her hands still soaking wet. Again, it beeps.

-- .- -- .-

(Mama)

Silence. Maria hurriedly fishes her phone from her pocket and types a message—soaping the keypad with her fingers. In the hospital, Maria's assistant is sitting beside Tenten in his room. Her phone beeps, and she checks the message.

How is he?

Maria's assistant types back.

Still asleep. Why?

Maria sends another message.

Alive?

Her assistant responds.

Yes. Why ???

Maria types.

Nothing. OK.

She slips her phone back in her pocket and sighs. She steadies herself—holding onto the table—and clutches the blue shawl around her neck. The radio, silent.

MARIA'S HOUSE. SUNSET.

After Maria finishes doing the chores, she gets ready to go back to the hospital. She glances out the window at the setting sun and takes a deep breath to prepare herself for the long night ahead. Maria then picks up her bag from the couch and switches the lights off in the living room. She's about to head for the door when the radio beeps again.

-- .- -- .-

(Mama)

This time, Maria leaps to the radio to pick it up, and her whole body freezes in anticipation. After a few seconds, the radio crackles in static and, in broken beeps, it relays another message.

.. / .-- .- -. - / - ---

(I want to)

She grips the radio in disbelief.

--. --- / .... --- -- .

(Go home)

This time, Maria lifts the radio up and walks around the room, trying to find a better signal— knocking down a lamp in the process.

-- .- -- .-

(Mama)

She goes out to the balcony, and the radio crackles again.

-.-. --- -- .

(Come)

Getting a better signal, the sequence of beeps repeats and then changes. Maria points the radio out toward the dusk sky—stepping on the railing of the balcony.

--. . - / -- .

(Get me)

Maria's eyes go wide, and, from her point of view as she's holding the radio up to the sky, she sees the twinkling stars in the dusk light. Her eyes focus on one star in particular as it flickers its faint light in the deepening darkness. Maria rushes back inside and, after a few moments, returns with a cardboard box. She rummages inside it and takes out a cylindrical object, thinking it's a telescope. Maria looks through the eyepiece and sees an iridescent burst of swirling colors. She takes another look at the toy and sees that it's a kaleidoscope. Annoyed, she throws it over her shoulder and rummages inside the box once again. After a second, she pulls out a pair of toy binoculars and brings them to her eyes, looking at the star through the milky lenses. Seeing it a little bit clearer now, she notices that the star is twinkling in constant yet staggered succession.

-- . - -- .-
(Mama)

.-- .- -. - / - ---
(Want to)

-.-. --- -- .
(Come)

.... --- -- .
(Home)

-.-. --- -- .
(Come)

--. . - / -- .
(Get me)

Maria stumbles back, her eyes still fixated on the twinkling star. Suddenly, her phone rings, demanding her attention.

Back in the hospital, the doctor and several nurses surround Tenten's bed. The doctor is performing chest compressions on him, and one nurse administers a shot to his arm. Rapid beeps can be heard filling the room. Maria's assistant is outside in the hallway—her phone pressed to her ear.

Maria answers the phone and, almost immediately, her lips begin to quiver. She covers her mouth with a shaking hand while holding back tears. Steadying herself, Maria takes another look at the twinkling star, and a flare of determination surfaces from within her. She knows exactly what she needs to do.

AVIATOR'S HOUSE. NIGHT.

The rapid and frustrated trilling of a doorbell goes off in the darkness. Tripping over the furniture as he navigates his living room, the retired aviator who recently visited Maria's Wash hurriedly opens the door. He is surprised to see Maria standing on the porch, panting. He greets her with a confused look as she begins to mutter, wildly gesturing with her hands, hysterical but surprisingly understandable. Then, a huge, proud grin spreads across the aviator's face. He nods.

FIELD. NIGHT.

Behind the wheel of a pickup truck, Maria looks straight ahead with unyielding resolve. Sitting in the passenger seat, the aviator adjusts his goggles—eyes twinkling with excitement. The truck skids down the road, headlights beaming forward. In its cargo bed is a large wicker basket, spacious enough for one person to get into, a huge compact sport sack, an industrial fan, and other odd contraptions. Maria honks the horn a couple of times to warn pedestrians of their swift oncoming.

Soon they reach the open fields at the outskirts of the city, and the two of them hurriedly leap off the truck. Maria's phone beeps, and she checks another message, the light from the screen illuminating the lines of distress on her face. With their time running out, she stuffs her phone back inside her pocket and walks to the rear of the truck. The aviator helps her unload their cargo, and, as they heave the last of the equipment onto the grass, Maria takes out Tenten's toy binoculars from her leather-strap bag to peer at the blinking star directly above them. All the while, gray monsoon clouds are fast approaching, claiming the celestials one by one.

They quickly roll out a giant length of fabric that is revealed to be a massive deflated balloon, splaying it out on the field. Then, the aviator hooks thick ropes from the wicker basket to the crumpled hem of the fabric envelope.

The industrial fan whirrs to life, sending blasts of air to the mouth of the giant balloon, and it slowly inflates on its side, getting bigger and bigger. Maria and the aviator hold the opening as wide as they can, and soon there's an entire chamber of air inside the giant balloon.

Flames shoot out like a focused torch from a propane tank protruding from the center of the wicker basket, still on its side. With a steady thrum and hiss of hot air, the balloon slowly lifts off the ground as it fills with heat. And Maria and the aviator let it rise as they adjust the wicker basket, turning it right side up.

Within moments, a towering hot air balloon stands in front of them, the aviator looking prouder than ever. Maria nods to him and proceeds to board the wicker basket with his help. Then, the aviator releases the ropes attaching the hot air balloon to the pickup truck, and it begins its ascent. Maria glances back at the aviator, and he thrusts his thumb in the air and winks. She nods, turns toward the propane tanks, and cranks up the heat. The flames burst in a pillar of fire upward, the hot-air balloon takes off, and Maria takes flight.

SKY. NIGHT.

The hot-air balloon rises up into the sky. Maria's phone beeps once again, but this time she doesn't check the message. Instead, she continues adjusting the course of the vessel, looking toward the sky with fierce resolve.

As Maria floats away, several people at the edge of the city point to the field—seeing the aircraft ascending. The lady in the burka, previously in Maria's Wash, gapes from her windowsill. A little girl tugs at her father's sleeve, and they both look at the lady flying a hot-air balloon toward the stratosphere.

The city lights shrink smaller and smaller, moving farther and farther away until they are no more than twinkling stars beneath her feet. In the distance, nimbus clouds thunder closer and closer as the balloon moves higher and higher. The wind around Maria picks up speed, but she remains steadfast.

The winds howl all around her as the storm pushes forth. The monsoon crashes against the hot-air balloon. Clouds come rolling in, engulfing her vessel. And Maria fights through the turbulence like a sailor battling the high seas.

Maria is battered by the powerful gales. Flashes of lightning illuminate the giant nimbi. Thunder rumbles everywhere. Maria holds tightly on the reins and braces herself against the tempest, her blue shawl flapping wildly around her neck. Then, the knot comes undone, and the shawl flies free as it gets caught in the rush of air. Maria grabs on tighter and shuts her eyes—grunting and yelping in desperate prayer every time a violent lash of wind beats its way through the balloon. But her cries are drowned out by the wind, water, and ice.

Then, like a vacuum opening up, air rushing out all at once: silence.

SKY. NIGHT.

Maria fearfully opens her eyes. She has passed through the storm. Hesitantly, she leans out from the wicker basket. All around her are rolls and rolls of clouds, like hills as far as she can see, softly shifting below the hot-air balloon, undulating like the foamy sea. Maria laughs to herself before deftly taking out her handheld radio and turning it on in one swift motion. The radio crackles to life. She turns the dial, and the radio emits a series of high-pitched whirrs and squeaks, followed by steady beeping, relaying,

-- .- -- .-

(Mama)

She stares at the radio. Again,

-- .- -- .-

(Mama)

-.-. --- -- .

(Come)

--. . - / -- .

(Get me)

She takes her flashlight from her bag and switches it on. She points it to the stars and flickers the light.

 - . -. / - . -.
 (Tenten)

A moment passes. The radio beeps again. Sound and light touch.

 .. / .- -- / .... . .-. .
 (I am here)

Maria smiles. Suddenly, the radio whirrs and drowns in static. She picks it up and shakes it desperately. The radio retches and spurts out high-pitched scratching before going completely silent. Maria bangs on the radio, hoping to make it work again, but to no avail. She begins to cry.

Then, a warm glow lights up Maria's face, caressing the tears streaming down her cheeks. She opens her eyes, and, from between the gaps in the weaving of the wicker, she glimpses a soft yellow light peeking through. Maria gets up and looks out from the wicker basket. There, about fifty meters away, she sees her son suspended in the air above the clouds, his clothes gently billowing in the wind. Tenten is shining like a small star, casting light on the clouds below. He's not alone; in the far distance, Maria can see several others, glowing motes of light hovering in the atmosphere.

Percy Eid

Maria stares at her son for a moment. She glances below and contemplates the strong winds churning the clouds under her feet. Not knowing what to do, Maria takes her flashlight and points it at her son. She flickers the light.

-.-./-..-.
(Tenten)

He looks at her. The radio crackles to life and beeps.

-- .- -- .- / -.-- --- ..- / -.-. .- -- .
(Mama you came)

Maria responds.

-.-- . .... / .. / -.-. --- -- . / --. . - / -.-- --- ..-
(Yes I come get you)

The sound of the radio beeping:

.-- .- -. - / - --- / -.-. --- -- . / .... --- -- .
(Want to come home)

The light from the flashlight blinking:

-.-- . .... / - . -. - . -. / -.-. --- -- . / .... --- -- .
(Yes Tenten come home)

Tears flow steadily down Maria's cheeks, but just as she tries to relay one more message, the balloon lurches.

Maria jerks forward and drops her flashlight. The howling wind rises all around her, rocking the basket. The last thing Maria sees before the clouds engulf her once again is Tenten smiling.

FIELD. NIGHT.

The aviator is listening to a song on the radio inside his pickup truck. Outside, the light rain pelts the metal roof and the windows of the vehicle. Through the glass, the world warps, marred by the cascading water. And yet, reflected on the windshield, a small object can be seen hurtling from the sky. The aviator looks up, sees the unidentified falling object, and sticks his head out for a better view. Recognition dawns on his face like cold rain, and in a panic, he starts the engine and stomps on the gas pedal. The truck starts, and the wheels skid through the wet grass, muddying the ground. The aviator drives across the field, swerving left and right while keeping track of the falling aircraft.

Up in the air, thousands of feet from the ground, the hot-air balloon manages to hold most of its structure against the battering of the wind. But the envelope has been damaged and is flapping in its descent, barely resisting the air and slowing down its fall. The aviator's eyes remain trained on his magnificent aircraft, now plummeting down to earth with a torn parachute valve.

The hot-air balloon, falling horizontally, strays to the nearby woods. It catches on a few trees, tearing through boughs and crowns, before it eventually tumbles to the ground. The wind weakens the impact of the crash and carries the envelope across the wide clearing as the balloon drags its splintered wicker basket through the grass. Finally, the balloon slows and settles.

The aviator catches up to the fallen aircraft, arriving where it crash-landed. He leaps out of the truck and runs toward the basket. He pushes the thick sheets, stray debris, and some tangled rope away to find the wicker basket busted open. There he sees its pilot: alive and breathing, dirty but miraculously unharmed. The aviator kneels beside Maria and nudges her. She stirs.

Slowly, Maria comes to and looks at the aviator, who smiles warmly at her. Maria is still disoriented but at the same time astonished that she survived. She pats herself all over her body, trying to assess the damage before letting out a big sigh of relief and lying down. She chuckles softly, and for a moment all the worry seems to have left her body. And then, jerking upright, she remembers.

HOSPITAL. DAWN.

Maria and the aviator race down the hospital hallway, making their way toward Tenten's room, and just as they round the corner, they run into Maria's assistant. She gasps at their sudden arrival, and Maria looks at her expectantly.

With all the courage left inside her, Maria opens the door to Tenten's room, her assistant and the aviator peeking over her shoulders. As the door opens wider, they see Tenten. He's in a half-sitting position, awake and chatting with a nurse. Maria bursts into the room, and Tenten looks at his mom. A big smile spreads across his face as he reaches his arms toward her. Maria dives in to hug her son tightly. She cups Tenten's face, squishing his cheeks and smothering him in quick kisses.

The doctor walks into the room distractedly scanning papers in his hands—earning him a strong pat on the back from the aviator, who laughs merrily as Maria's assistant gives him a grateful hug.

Outside, the sun begins to rise. And caught on a tree branch within view of the hospital window is a blue shawl flapping gently in the wind.

FIDO IN THE NIGHT - BY JOHN Q McDONALD

All those habitable planets in the known universe, and I'm stuck on the only one without an interstellar lifeboat, Steve whispered to himself. He intended the thought, also, for the darkness that spread around him, beneath the catwalk and around the observatory dome, darkness that hung above him and over the layer of softly glowing clouds lapping at the base of the mountain. A coyote laughed somewhere in the shadows, which felt to Steve like an appropriate retort to the wry expression that crept unseen across his face.

He gazed at the sky, picturing to himself the scattered positions of planets strewn across the deep blue-black between the few familiar stars he could see from the mountaintop. His mind's eye saw a star map with coordinates and grids. The air below him was choked with light and smoke, but this place remained the darkest spot left on the continent. There was a particularly juicy solar system just there, to the right of Orion's knee. It had three glittering little Earths.

So many from which to choose, Steve thought, *so many square miles of untouched landscape. Animals unhunted, unthreatened, unexterminated.*

A door hinge creaked. A triangle of light fell across the platform and the toes of his shoes.

"We still have half an hour of darkness to go, Stevie," said a small voice that cracked around his name.

"Yes," he said. "Thanks, Sharon." His eyes responded to the light, which cast the night back into formless void, leaving it to the wide-eyed coyotes and their shivering prey.

People tended to think Steve a cynic. He did have a sharp tongue and was not easily impressed, but he loved the night, and he enjoyed his supporting role in discovering the planets. A garage full of amateur astronomers and whiz-kid engineers in Boise had finally developed the ultra-high-resolution coronagraph/spectrograph after the professionals had spent decades making longer and longer catalogs of planets without knowing what any of them were really like. The Boise gadget allowed observers like Steve to detect oxygen and eventually chlorophyll in the atmospheres of faraway worlds. On a few, some claimed to discover the signature of animal skin cells drifting in the upper reaches of alien skies. A new satellite, properly a pair of satellites, was being prepared based upon the gadget. If it worked, it would further deepen the knowledge of these still barely known worlds.

On one, just one, there was scant but convincing evidence of the early stages of some animal's efforts to alter its environment. A civilization was revealed by the smoke it emitted. Back here on Earth, the sky was filled with smoke. People burned anything to survive. This was no longer a planet for an astronomer. Steve had tried to parlay his observations into a job on the satellite project, but the demand for those jobs was just too high, and they went to those most skilled at communicating with bureaucrats—not to cynics like Steve.

The source of Steve's latest anxieties, however, was entirely terrestrial. So it was mildly aggravating that there was as yet no spaceship, no hyperdrive to the stars. He wished he could take that ride, even if the air the aliens breathed was pure chlorine. He just wanted to go.

The scratched voice that called him in from the darkness belonged to a small woman with short, bouncy blond hair, sneakers with holes in the soles, and bright, earnest eyes. Sharon was childlike; Steve couldn't quite accept that she was a little older and presumably wiser. She ran the observatory on nights like this, not letting Steve touch the scientific equipment his fat grant money had actually paid for. Her tiny voice belied the stubborn competence of Sharon's work.

As he fell into the chair in front of the arc of the computer screens, he caught from her what seemed to be an appraising glance. She was watching him. They were *all* watching him. They were subtle about it, or tried to be, but he was too quick for them. He could tell. And he wasn't paranoid. He endured a kind of perpetual probation. Try to kill yourself just once, and they never stop watching you, wanting to be there to get a good look should you try it again.

"Ready to proceed?" Sharon asked. Her voice was both stronger and struck with that blasted concern.

"As I'll ever be," he said. Sharon registered that it wasn't just the work he was talking about.

Steve watched as she worked the keyboard, slewing the telescope to point at another of the bright stars he studied from there. He saw her imagine the spectacle of him jamming a needle into his carotid artery. And yet she hummed to herself, quietly.

And it hadn't been a bad idea, at that, he thought. In the ten hours between administering the drug to himself and the shocking moment when he awoke in intensive care, he had endured the most profound, pleasant, and *timeless* experience of his life. It was a wink of an eye, eternity in a measureless moment, an utter and terrible void. But he couldn't tell Sharon that. He couldn't describe, for anyone, the bliss and terror of ten hours of death.

They might have just left me there, he thought. *But now that I'm back, I want to stay.* That was as much to say, too, that he wanted to climb aboard the next available flying saucer and fly away to the immense forgetfulness of an alien planet.

"So," Sharon said, in a voice that snapped Steve from his thoughts, "what are you going to do when you're done with your shift?"

Steve looked at the back of her head, as she looked back and forth from the keyboard to the shining screen in front of her. "Thought I might go fishing," he said.

Sharon laughed a tight kind of painful laugh. "Fish," she said. "I'd kill to have some nice seared tuna."

"Jeez," he said, "that was quick. You must be carrying a dream of sushi around with you."

"Oh sure, and you don't remember the things you wish you could have again?" She cut herself off on the edge of another question.

Steve looked at her. She had turned toward him. He noticed her panicked expression, but it calmed as she looked at him. "I do," he said, "of course. Apples."

"Apples?"

"Apples. Pears. Any autumn fruit, bright and wet with cool moisture." He raised his eyebrow at how this might have sounded. There was a short pause.

"Well," she said, swallowing her nerves. "You're certainly not going fishing. So, what *are* you up to?"

"Tinkering in the garage and counting needles on the cactus in the yard," he said. "Nothing much." *Building my own private spaceship,* he thought. Now that he had decided not to kill himself after all, he had to find *something* to do with his time.

After a moment, he looked back at her. She was still sitting there, looking at him. The computer clicked away at the data from the telescope that purred in the next room. "What about you?" he asked.

"Killing time. You know, hanging out. There's a get-together on Friday at the Sandia. Just some friends."

Friday was an anniversary. The Sandia was Diana's favorite bar. What the hell was Sharon thinking? *"Killing time," for Christ's sake,* Steve thought. *Couldn't she just follow everyone's advice about talking to me?*

But in the moment it didn't really bother him. What bothered him was how much all of it bothered everybody else.

o

ONE NIGHT, SIX MONTHS BEFORE, HE WAS ALONE ON the mountain with Diana's lifeless body. They had worked together on the planet-finding project for two years. She was his fiancée, or she might have been if he had ever worked up the courage to give her the moonstone ring he'd bought months before. But it didn't work out that way, and the altitude of the mountain had fallen upon her weak heart, pulled a plug, and filled her lungs with fluid. The pulmonary edema came on quick and strong, and Steve panicked. He thought she was having a heart attack, which didn't make sense, since she was only twenty-six. He tried the halting steps of CPR he could remember when she fell silent after she had gasped for air and complained of the chest pain. All he accomplished was to aggravate the edema, and she soon drowned in her own fluids. The doctor tried to tell him it wasn't his fault, but he couldn't escape the sense that he had pushed her out of this world. The woman he loved, after years of looking for her. It was the kind of thing that could drive a man to suicide.

They had been sitting together in the control room, talking about the planets they had discovered as though they were their children.

"How about Fido?" he said.

"You'd name your kid like he was a dog?" Diana replied, her eyebrows raised. She had black hair, black eyes, black humor, and a shrewd nature.

"Well, we're talking hypothetically, aren't we?"

"Choose wisely. The naming committee might take your recommendation and name it whatever you want. Besides, this is *our kid* you're talking about."

His heart stirred at her choice of words. Diana rubbed gently at a spot near the middle of her chest. She had a thoughtful look on her face.

"It's a planet," he said, "not a baby."

"Then stick with HD36485B."

"Fido has a better ring to it."

She smiled a strained smile.

"Are you okay?" he asked.

Twenty minutes later, Diana was gone.

○

ON FRIDAY, HE FOUND HIMSELF WALKING DOWN A quiet street toward the Sandia. He had, indeed, spent time in his garage, with its door open to the desert air that flowed over him like a silken blanket. Steve imagined himself working on the mechanisms for spaceflight, but he had never been one of those high-tech tinkerers like the guys who built the spectrograph he used on the mountain. He messed with low-tech hardware reminiscent of the models he built when he was a kid. It kept his fingers busy, and the dexterity required was a safe place into which he could retreat. This week, he worked on his neighbor's lawn mower. Steve never saw much point to a lawn here in the desert, especially the few hundred square feet next door, a patch the neighbor nurtured jealously against the combined elements of desert heat, absurdly expensive water, and community disapprobation.

He hummed "Clair de Lune" to himself as he walked down the road. Steve failed to reflect on the mild contentment that this indicated. Most of the time, the very idea of contentment seemed too bizarre to contemplate. When he did think about his mood, he returned often to those fugitive ten hours of oblivion and concluded that this world wasn't about happiness or sadness, but the indifference of an incomprehensible void. On the face of it, it didn't really make sense to worry, but he worried.

The Sandia was a wide covered deck with cheerful light surrounding a bungalow on a dark road on the edge of town. Steve and Diana had shared many mediocre pizzas and lots of decent beer here. Diana said it reminded her of happy summers on wide porches beside New England lakes. He liked to see her enjoying herself, head thrown back and shoulders dropped, reveling in warm memories. Now, of course, the place was haunted.

And yet he found himself at the door of the Sandia, looking across a room full of people, all about his age, talking over loud music, drinking and spilling beer in equal amounts, at tables spaced widely along the walls. The ceiling was hung with a chaos of desert ranch equipment, a jumble of rust and wood worn gray with age.

He stood a moment, shoulder leaning against the doorframe, and gazed around the room. The group from the observatory sat at a long table, and those facing him smiled and nodded. Steve stepped to the bar and bought a beer. The Sandia was the only place he knew that would serve a stout warm, and that discovery had made it almost as precious to him as it was to Diana. The bartender, though, always claimed the beer was warm just to save a little energy.

They looked up at him as he stepped to the table.

"Hey, Steve," said David.

"Sharon said you might come by," said George.

"She isn't here yet?" Steve asked.

"Nope," David said, gulping his beer, "but she should be along soon."

"What's the occasion?"

There was an awkward pause. "It's an anniversary, isn't it?" Lisa asked. She sat at a corner of the table, almost hidden behind the men. The only reason Steve heard her was that the music had grown quiet for a moment.

He gulped the air. Anniversary. A year ago, on the balcony of the observatory dome, he had kissed Diana for the first time. He felt his eyes cross. *How could they know that?*

"The first habitable planet we found with that spectrograph," said David. "It's been two years. Now we've got hundreds!"

"Thousands," Lisa whispered.

David glanced at her. Steve felt a well of sympathy for Lisa and the quiet place she held in the organization. But he was speechless. The tune in his head vanished, replaced by the sound of a human voice, Diana's, in a jumble of words, whispers, and her cooing laughter.

David turned to Steve. "What's up, man?"

Then all of their faces were on him.

Steve placed his beer on the table. The concern that grew in their eyes pushed his mood backward into a wave of regret. He couldn't stand those looks of pity. They didn't know what was going on. None of them knew the void he had seen up close, and not the one at the end of a telescope.

"Steve?"

He looked down at the creamy surface of his beer. His fingers trembled.

"It's nothing," he stammered. "I'm fine." He turned away from the table, murmuring, "I'm just going to go back and get some fresh air."

David made to go after him, but Lisa stopped him with a hand laid on his arm.

In the darkness just beyond the puddle of light cast from strings of porch lights, Steve ran almost headlong into Sharon. She approached on the same road he had come down and was looking up at the sky when he collided with her.

He veered to one side and danced on one foot to avoid pushing her over.

"Jeez, Stevie, what's the big hurry?" she asked.

"Taking a walk," he said, distracted.

"Hey, wait," she said. "I had no idea you'd be here. It's good to see you."

"It's an anniversary," he said.

"Yes, I know," she said with a small laugh in her voice. "Two years." She reached up and kissed him on the cheek, a kiss that lingered there just a touch longer than mere friendship.

"No," he said, his head spinning. "No, you don't really know. But that's okay." He laid a hand on her shoulder. "They're waiting for you. I need some air."

She cast that same piteously worried look up at his face, and he found himself disgusted by it. He knew he should feel grateful, some appreciation for all this concern for his well-being. These people cared about him. He didn't like knowing that, but it wasn't a bad thing. Right now, though, waves of grief rose in his chest like bile and burned in his throat. He was on the verge of vomiting out the one sip of stout he'd had in the bar.

"Some air," Sharon said, finally, nodding. "Sure, sure, you need your space."

"I do," he gasped. "For a few minutes, at least."

"Everybody already here?"

"I don't know who everybody should be, but there are folks in there. Having a good time by the looks of it." He tried to sound light, but his voice trailed off. The bile began to sink.

"Okay," she said. "I'll see you later?"

It was a question he couldn't answer in that moment. Blackness enfolded him from the star-dotted sky above. "Yeah," he said. "Go on in."

Sharon turned and walked across the road. An ancient Volkswagen bug whistled by. He turned and headed the other way, away from the lights of the city.

o

"OUCH," DIANA WHISPERED. AND A MOMENT LATER she whispered, "Nothing."

These were her last two words. *Ouch … Nothing …* By the time the paramedics arrived at the observatory, she was dead, staring blankly at the insides of her eyelids and into whatever unknowable darkness or light there might have been.

Steve had rolled up her hand-knitted scarf under her head and laid her jacket over her body. There was a heart-shaped pin on the lapel. His heart hadn't slowed, his head hurt, but there was nothing he could do. A droplet of blood was drying at the corner of her mouth, and he resisted the urge to kiss it away. When there was a loud knock at the door, he was chilled to the bone.

It was warm on the road out of town, away from the Sandia, and the stars twinkled through the haze in the sky. Orion was there again, the brightest stars in his shoulders and knees, the belt faint. Steve could see the pavement and the double yellow line by the faint light of the haze illuminated by city lights and by whatever starlight made it to the ground.

A car passed, blinding him for a moment, and moving silently. *Electric,* he thought. *Electricity keeps our brains working.* The thought was incongruous, but it was something Diana would have said. Another, noisier car passed. He stopped on the road and listened as his eyes readjusted to the darkness.

Silence.

Thanks to sprawl and the toxic cloud of civilization, the sky couldn't be totally black anymore. Nothing was truly dark in the sky. But he knew real darkness was not only dark but empty. *Ten hours of it,* he thought, *or an eternity.*

He walked awhile longer. The road stretched out straight in front of him until it passed between low hills on the horizon. Steve wasn't sure how long he walked. After some time, he noted a brightening light on the horizon, just where the road disappeared between the hills. *Another car, no doubt,* he thought. He stepped out of the road and stood by a rock with two or three saguaro standing nearby. A few minutes passed, and no car came, but the light continued to grow. It shone bluish against the brownish tinge of the haze, and it began to take on a distinctive shape.

By now, Steve's eyes were well-adjusted to the night. He knew from experience on the mountain that this would make him more sensitive to what lay out there in the sky, whatever wasn't obscured by the smoke from oil well fires and faraway disasters he didn't want to name. Cacti were silhouetted against the growing light on the horizon. Finally, a sliver of almost white light rose at the end of the road. With the shape of the hills to either side, it looked like a flying saucer seen edge-on. For a moment, Steve indulged the fantasy and saw the light there approaching, soaring low over the desert to scoop him up and take him to HD36485B... Fido, somewhere far away among all those planets.

Steve's illusion dissolved as the moon made its way into the sky, somewhere past full, bent and bluish-orange in the thick air at the edge of the world.

He smiled. He even let out a little laugh. *Diana,* he thought, *the Moon,* and there were tears in his eyes, too.

o

AN HOUR AND MORE HAD PASSED WHEN HE RETURNED to the vicinity of the Sandia. The waning moon had risen into a yellowish haze behind him, casting a wan light along the road and the bushes behind the bar. Some of the lights had been turned off, and a few patrons nursed drinks on the tables along the porch railing. It was still before eleven, but most folks now kept early hours, conserving energy, so that the peak party hours were usually between four and ten, when, in the summer, some twilight could still be relied upon to keep the custom moving.

Nothing, he thought, again, and for the thousandth time, in Diana's voice. "Nothing at all," he whispered to himself as he reached the bottom of the steps.

Sharon sat alone at a table by the door. An empty pint glass was on the table in front of her, and a highball glass with about half a finger of a sweet-looking brown liquid. Hearing his footsteps, she looked up at Steve and gave him a weak smile, though the upward twitch in her eyebrows suggested she was genuinely happy to see him.

"Steve," she rasped, her voice thick with tiredness. "Sit with me."

He slid into the chair across from her.

"Where'd you go?" she said. "Gone so long."

"Needed the walk, I guess," he said. "Didn't know I'd take so much time."

"That's okay," she said. "David was telling us about some of the latest processed data. Even more promising than you'd think. Another few weeks of observing, and we might be able to go public."

"Public? With what?"

"You know," she said. "Fido, you call it. Real signs of something intelligent altering its environment. Fire smoke. Compound chemicals." Sharon tried to sound excited, but there was something missing from her voice.

His thoughts returned, finally, to the moment. *Nothing*, he thought, *indeed*.

"Aren't you excited?" she asked.

"Sure," he said. "Of course. I can't imagine what the rest of the world will think. Especially these days."

"What do you mean?"

"Everyone will want to go there. Meet their alien brethren. Lay waste to that planet, too."

"Think so?" She gulped the last sip of her drink. "If these data are right, they've already started down that road."

"Give 'em a few millennia," he said. His voice trailed off. He looked at her, caught her eye for the first time, glinting in the light of the porch lights. A shadow cast by the building lay across the patch of gravel. Moonlight tinted the needles of a lone tree. "What?" said Steve. "There's something else."

"There's something else," said Sharon. "How observant, actually, are you?"

"To be honest, I've been having a hard time with that lately."

"Well, let me clarify things for you, then."

He felt a tumble in his gut—surprise—and a stirring in his heart.

Sharon pushed her glasses to the side, leaving a wet streak on the polished surface of the table. "No point in being oblique. Hasn't worked. Wasn't going to work." She closed her eyes for a moment. Shook her head. "I hope it isn't only the drink talking, Steve, but you have to know I've developed some serious feelings for you."

Steve wasn't really caught off guard. The signs were there, but his emotions wouldn't respond. "Yes?" he said. "I think I've been observant enough for that. But dead inside, you know? I mean, shit…"

"I don't want to cause trouble," she said. "It's obvious things aren't easy. But I wanted you to consider me as a potential stepmother."

"Stepmother? What?"

"To Fido. I know Diana…"

He lifted a hand to his brow. Sharon leaned down and looked up at his eyes.

"I know Diana," she began again, "and you considered that planet your pet project. Your baby, if you will."

"Yes."

"Let me take over with you. Let me adopt your baby. I loved Diana, too, in my own way."

Steve looked at her. The warmth in his heart continued to grow. He felt released. It was suddenly easy for him to imagine Diana letting go of his hand, waving goodbye. *Nothing,* he heard her whisper. *Nothing but now,* he thought. His hand slid across the table, his fingertips touching Sharon's.

"Is there any way, you think, we could keep Fido to ourselves? Just a little longer?" he asked.

"I don't know," she said. "You know how kids are. You do what you can for them, and then they've got to live a life of their own."

"Thank you," he said. "But be patient with me. I'm a little unhinged."

"Anyone living in this world would have to be."

Steve awoke alone the next morning. For the first time since Diana's body was driven away from the mountaintop, he felt her presence had receded. He knew the love endured, but the weight of loss had begun to fall away. He looked at a picture on the wall. His dog when he was a kid. Not a lot of people kept dogs anymore. His name was Squint. "It'll be okay with you, too, won't it boy?"

THE PARCHMENT - BY ANDY BETZ

I AWOKE COLD AND SOMEWHAT HUNGRY. MY SURVEY OF MY ROOM WAS QUICK, THE CONTENTS WERE FEW. MEASURING FIVE METERS BY THREE METERS, THE room had a cot, a small table, and a chair. On the table, I found a parchment with hand-drawn letters. It was not writing, more like different letters from different sources, more of a ransom note in appearance. Its message was clear.

Through the door but once.

Cooler heads prevail there.

You will be contacted soon.

Having no food and no water, I had no choice. The door looked common, but my imagination thought it was not. I searched for a trap or a camera recording my every move. I found none. Waiving the inevitable hours of being perplexed, I gripped the door handle, opened the door, and entered.

What I found was not what I expected. My room adjoined a small, open-floor, house-sized chamber. In it was a much larger bed, a food pantry, a bookshelf full of titles, a bathroom, a kitchen, and accommodations for exactly one. In my wonderment, I released the door handle. As promised, the door closed and locked from the other side. I felt air expand into the room, bringing it to a positive pressure before I began my inventory.

There were no windows and no manner in which to escape. I had limited electricity available to me. I assumed holding tanks for discharged water from cooking, cleaning, and sanitary requirements were my only plumbing source. My pantries were filled with foodstuffs, water, other beverages, and clothing for me. In all, I was sealed in a room in which I was to make myself comfortable. The furnishings were from early-twentieth-century North America, and perishables were in quantities to last nearly six days at my consumption rate.

Since I was designed to remain captive and uninformed of my surroundings for quite some time, I found a copy of *The Count of Monte Cristo*, a glass of whiskey, and a comfortable spot on my bed, and then I sat for a long time, reading and of course sleeping.

For the first time in ages, I dreamed of returning to Earth, seeing it as I remember it, before the war, as early explorers saw it, as all people should see it.

When I awoke, my head hurt, maybe due to a hangover, maybe due to a bad dream. My glass was empty, the book barely started. What was new was the parchment on the table.

You will receive new rations every two standard periods.

Please plan accordingly.

Every four increments, respond in writing to written questions.

When the parchment appeared is not as important as how the parchment appeared. Finding no portal, I had to conclude that someone was watching me, waiting for an opportunity to enter my confines. Whether they (or him or her or … ?) wanted me for benevolent or nefarious reasons remained unclear. What was clear was that I was imprisoned in a cage, somewhat of a luxury, but a cage nonetheless. All I had to do was bide my time and wait. I had no other pressing engagements to divert me from my appointment.

It took, by my internal clock, three days until I had my answer. I feigned sleep with a whiskey glass nearby. I thought it was a dream that I saw. I thought it couldn't be real. In the morning (how would I know it was morning?) on the third day, I saw a beam of dull light transport a being to a spot adjacent to my table. When it reached over to place a parchment on the table, I jumped from my bed to grab the form in the light. It succeeded. I failed. As if I did not exist, the being offered no corporeal resistance as I passed through what I thought was a solid form. It continued to lower the parchment, paused, and then beamed out of sight. I spent the next day nursing a bruised arm (impact with the table) and needing that whiskey more than ever.

It took a day before I even read the parchment. This time, it said:

> *It is in your best interest to remain calm.*

> *Respond in writing.*

> *Do you have any inventory requirements?*

> *Are you injured or in need of medical assistance?*

> *Can you be patient in waiting for a reply?*

Once I read it, I took the pen (felt like some type of electronic stylus) and began to write. My answers were brief and to the point. As soon as I'd finished writing, *no, no,* and *yes,* the parchment disappeared in the same beam of dull light as before—this time without the illusion of an intelligent presence. Then it was back to *The Count of Monte Cristo* for a minimum of three days and nights. Back to learning about rationing my stores until I understood what two standard periods were. Back to waiting for a reply that part of me hoped would never arrive.

The reply took too long to come for me to have kept accurate records of elapsed time, other than from the growth of my beard and the molding of a single slice of bread. After what I believed was three days, the beam of light returned with the "holographic" being. I showed him no interest. He returned my indifference with patience. After two hours, I sat up from the bed.

I never even had the chance to begin speaking. The being started a written conversation.

You are at the far side of Deimos 2, in isolation, for your safety.

There are no other lifeforms on this station.

You know the war between us and the Tratos is all but lost.

Earth is still occupied.

Please remain calm.

You are humanity's last hope.

The parchment is our only form of communication.

Take your time to answer my questions.

Will you comply?

I wrote the word *yes* on the parchment. Seconds later, the being faded into a light blue haze, similar to its first departure. I awaited a new series of questions.

I didn't have to wait for long.

We need your assistance desperately.

You are the only remaining human not cataloged by the Tratos.

Not that they couldn't find you.

Only because you couldn't be cataloged.

Do you still have headaches?

I used the pen to write, *not anymore.* With that, the being showed the briefest of smiles.

Good.

And Bad.

This makes you dangerous to their entire species, because you give hope to all of ours.

We need you to remain calm at all times.

If you become agitated for any reason, you become trackable.

Then you become dead.

Do you understand?

Back to the pen to confirm I understood what he wanted. I just didn't understand why he wanted it.

Now, I will answer the questions you have yet to ask.

We (and that is all the identification you will receive) smuggled you off Earth.

That was two Earth years ago.

You will not remember this event or any part of the war.

We have purged it from your mind for your safety.

You have been in stasis until six of your (human) days ago.

You have a gene that helps render you immune to excitement.

Two centuries ago, this caused what was known as a poker face.

If you have questions, please do not speak.

Please write them.

I let him have all that I had. It took me nearly thirty minutes to write them all on the parchment. Most of what I wanted to know, I knew they would not want to answer. Ironically, what they wanted to know about me they must have already known. The only question that remained was what was I to do?

We need you to remain calm and wait.

Every time you touch something, we collect your DNA.

Every time you breathe, we collect your DNA.

This is how we can win.

When we have collected enough, we will replicate what we need.

We will splice your gene into all of the remaining two million humans.

Then we will be immune to Tratos tracking.

Then we will attack!

Humanity may not win.

But humanity will have a chance.

I waited ten minutes for another order. It never came. He, however, departed, leaving the pen and the parchment on the table. I waited for hours for his return.

The next time I awoke, I had new rations in the pantry and all of the time on my hands to finish *The Count of Monte Cristo* before beginning *War and*

Peace. If this was my part of the war effort, so be it. I don't remember anything about a war, but being here beats prison any day, any time. I think.

The last ration arrived two weeks later. My ship (cell?) powered up for what I believe was a trans-phasic pulse message that overloaded the last of the station's power cores. I encountered the darkness before the cold. Either way, the lack of oxygen would have killed me. Alone, no one would know how I aided in the war effort. Millions have died in obscurity before me. Millions will die in the same fashion in the years to come. That is the way of all wars.

I could only hope the message made it in time to make a difference during this one.

Something told me I might be right. I was paying a high price for my hunch.

SOMEWHERE NEAR THE TRATOS HOME WORLD, A research station received an encoded trans-phasic pulse message.

Ref: Deimos 2 Research Lab Final Report

Have collected sufficient material for human eugenics weaponry.

Samples to arrive soon.

Begin assembly of transport systems.

Andy Betz

Prediction: 98% human fatality rate in 1 standard period for humans occupying Tratos.

Prediction: 75% human fatality rate in 6 standard periods for humans on Earth.

Prediction: All humans dead within 20 standard periods.

Begin immediate transport of select Tratos personnel to Earth for colonization.

End of Message.

TEACHING AN OLD DOLPHIN NEW TRICKS - BY TIMOTHY C GOODWIN

ROSETTA WASN'T MEAN: SHE HAD SIMPLY DEVELOPED AN ALOOFNESS, A CONTENTIOUSNESS. A CRUST. SHE HAD BEEN WORKING IN SPACE FOR TWENTY YEARS, and with that kind of experience, you get a little set in your ways.

So it wasn't that she hated *The Galloping Dolphin*. It was just that the ship was too nice, too modern. Too clean. Open-plan decks? Private cabins (with *beds*!) for the crew? Something called The Softening Room? Nope: she didn't trust it. Rosetta had cut her teeth on rust-infected, asteroid-beaten, peeled-aluminum death traps where sleeping quarters were modified/unmodified cargo holds, computer and toilet breakdowns were the norm, and the kitchen doubled as the gym. And the shower. And the astrocartography station.

Not to mention her crewmates: a boatload of children. She was used to one "Captain" and anywhere from five to twenty assholes who thought they knew better. But here, these kids were chatting, giggling, bubbling, fawning, laughing, just having a grand old time playing *Whoop! There Goes the Rock!* with each other on those stupid sKreenies, making friendship pixels for each other, and hooking up.

But she needed the gig, and Garrosson knew someone who knew someone, et cetera, et cetera, et cetera, who could get her aboard the Dolphin Interplanetary Logistics Corporation's newest flagship, hauling toothpaste or some shit out to the F-ring. Go corporate? Rosetta shuddered at the thought but tried to use the old "a contract is a contract" reasoning, until she realized that this bright ship with its freshly baked crew would *never* listen to her. Years of experience, underutilized.

That is, until today.

Today, *The Galloping Dolphin* was on fire.

And not only *that*, but Billsie was missing.

○

THE FIRST VICTIM OF THE FIRE WAS CHOOBLIE, THE ship's AI babysitter. Everyone had "duties," but Chooblie actually ran it all; he was the kind of sentient that used omni-directional speakers so they could sound like they were just behind you, cheery like a serial killer reading you a bedtime story. Chooblie wanted to watch movies with you. Asked you if you would like another crêpe. Said they were always ready and willing to chat, buddy-to-buddy.

Rosetta couldn't stand it.

"Hello, my little dolphins," Chooblie said, having called everyone to the bridge. "An announcement: The Softening Room has three new dandelions available on Tuesday. If you need to get railed, let me know! Now. Unfortunately, I have some news: a fire has broken out in the— Oh, my—"

The crew stood on the bridge, waiting for Chooblie as if he had simply stepped away to take a phone call.

The Captain, a great doofus of a dingus, called out, "Chooblie?"

Nothing.

The Captain, whose parents had *no doubt* paid for his position, called out, "Choobers?"

Nothing.

The Captain, who pressed his work suit, called out, "Choochoo—"

"Chooblie is dead," Rosetta said, laced with the tone of *you jackass*.

The crew turned to look at her.

She put her hands on her hips, snorted a laugh. "Looks like those colonists are gonna have to wait for their toothpaste."

The crew looked at each other, then back at her.

"Tooth … paste?" Marsi said.

"Yeah. *Tooth … paste.* You know, our cargo?"

"We're hauling Velirium Daxite," Traceo said, with that perpetual *as-if* face of hers. "Two hundred thousand metric tons of Velirium Daxite."

Rosetta stood straight. There was a slight pause that her nervous system filled with some tight head shaking and a few blinks. "What?"

"We're hauling Velirium Daxite," Traceo repeated, crossing her arms with that ... ohhh, Rosetta *hated* that face.

"Didn't you read the ... manifest?" Marsi said.

Rosetta quickly stepped to the backup ops station, the one with an actual lettersboard and screen wand, and began frantically clacking away to find out about this fire for herself.

The Galloping Dolphin was a slot-loader. Imagine a giant skyscraper with wings on top. The wings? Five decks for the crew, plus one Superlaunch X-12 Fold Engine at the tip of each wing. The skyscraper part? That was where they kept the cargo.

Rosetta wandered through screens, every one adding more and more bad news. The Fire was taking full advantage of its bazillion-to-one shot of smithereening the ship into whatever is smaller than atoms. It had broken out in the starboard engine's Hemlok-9 Nano-Sash. Sent a flashback through the sub-thimm pressure binder (that was how it got Chooblie), and that, well, of course, down-booted the oxygen repeaters. If the repeaters couldn't mash the lockup of the vapor transfer valves, it would slowly but surely make its way to the cargo hold.

Where—surprise—there were two hundred thousand metric tons of the most flammable, volatile, petulant explosive substance ever created in a lab: Velirium Daxite. There was one-sixteenth of a teaspoon in each of *The Galloping Dolphin*'s engines, and that alone would keep the ship running for ten years.

Now, there isn't a spacer alive who doesn't like a little drama. Space is a very, very big ocean, and anything that breaks the monotony of delivering cargo to random outposts, stations, and vanity colonies is welcome. Personnel drama is the easiest: you put anywhere from five to twenty people making minimum wage in a tin can with a food processor that makes their food taste like farts? Conflict will happen. Mechanical drama is also pretty standard, and Rosetta had her share of glazed anecdotes where her keen thinking saved the crew—anecdotes that increased the actual dangers faced by roughly 12.3 percent every subsequent time she told them.

But *no one* wants to abandon ship.

"Abandon ship," Rosetta said. Her mouth was dry.

The crew looked at each other, then back at her.

The Captain, who had probably been given *everything* he ever wanted in his life, said, "Okayyy—"

"*ABANDON SHIP*," she clapped, as if they were a children's Hoopsla team. "Let's go [*Clap*] let's go

[*Clap*] suit up [*Clap*] let's go let's GOOO—[*Clap clap clap*]—OOO."

"Wait wait wait WAIT!"

The crew (including Rosetta) looked at … whatever his name was. The squeaky one.

"Where's Billsie?"

o

ROSETTA WOULDN'T BE CAUGHT *dead* IN THE SPACE suits Dolphin Logistics had provided for the crew: skintight and teal, with a little floppy fin on the back. She was in her trusty Yorklaussen, now in its fifteenth year of service as her white-and-orange personal looser-fit space suit. It had big pockets on the outside for tools, small pockets on the inside for snacks.

Since it was so old, her Tele-tru Comms Dot couldn't connect with the Dolphin suits' newer Zappa-Z Comm-Points, which she was happy for as she strapped Captain Dingdong into his seat in the escape pod: she couldn't hear his babbling. Not that she needed to. Every single captain—*every single one*—used this moment for that alpha-dork down-with-the-ship shit. And every single time—*every single time*—their eyes told the truth. And this one here? His eyes said he'd rather be poolside at mummy and duddy's moon cabana, drinking margaritas until he inherited their wealth.

Pulling his final strap tight, maybe with a little too much oomph, Rosetta could see her face reflected in his face shield.

He was so young.

She stepped back from the Captain, who threw his hands up in defeat. Rosetta suppressed a smirk. *No show-roics from you today,* she thought. She moved to the hatch of the escape pod and turned around to look at them all.

Wide-eyed. Staring.

She remembered Garrosson convincing her about the gig: "These kids will need someone like you. Be a teacher."

She put her hands on her hips. "A smooth sea never made a skilled sailor," she said, but the strapped-in, teal-colored crewlings all pointed to their helmets, giving the interplanetary hand signal for *I can't hear you.* "Shit," she said, angry at herself for forgetting. Then, "I'll get Billsie." And they all made the hand signal again, because again, the comms-thing, and Rosetta cursed more stridently, stepped out of the pod, closed the hatch, coded it, and *poof*: they were off, motoring to Russell Station, the closest haven.

The brats. Even if they could hear her, they wouldn't have listened. She had tried, *really tried,* to give them the benefit of her experience: suggestions based on countless contracts, countless coworkers, countless ships, but all of it, ignored. Shrugged off. Dismissed. This lesson, though? Space is dangerous, not a pleasure cruise? Ohhh, this was a lesson they were gonna learn, and they'd learn it from her.

And of *course* the missing crew member would be Billsie: Most Likely to Receive a Wedgie for the rest of their life. No one knew where the ship's youngest/biggest bookworm was. The ship's regular comms were tied into Chooblie, so no-go there. She'd had the squeaky one try to contact him through their inter-spacesuit comms as they were piling into the escape pod, and she'd even tried the old shouting-his-name: nothing.

She liked Billsie, mainly because he paid attention to her, gave her the respect that was woefully lacking from the rest of these waifs. But even if the missing crew member had been, say, Traceo, Rosetta would have gone back for them: spacers don't leave anyone behind. Another lesson. Everyone—*everyone*—Rosetta had ever worked with followed this unwritten rule.

Except, maybe, Abbana. He'd shove his own grandma out of the way to save himself.

Or Tuski, *that* self-centered asshole—

Point is, she would. Rosetta was the type of person who would.

Her plan was simple: find Billsie (five decks: how hard could it be?), kick open an airlock (one on each deck), stuff him and herself into an Emergency Space Tent (with its 2.4dmf-band homing beacon), watch *The Galloping Dolphin* put on the biggest fireworks display since the Big Bang, and enjoy some space float for … what? Two, three weeks, tops?

Okay. So. Rosetta was on the top deck, at the front of the ship, in the main hallway that ran the length of the ship. She turned around from the escape pod hatch and looked down the expansive seafoam green central hallway to the back of the ship, to the yellow handrail that went down to the next level, the cabins. She had no doubt: Billsie was in his cabin, probably wrapped around his favorite book, trying not to poop his pants.

She looked at her Wristy, opened up its timer. If The Fire acted like it should, she figured she had … mmm, twenty minutes. Since fires *never* act like they should, she subtracted ten minutes. Plus, unforeseen whatevers and a minute or two to coax this kid away from fear-driven paralysis … four minutes.

She set a timer for four minutes, an eternity, and, after looking out a porthole to see the bright star that was the escape pod motoring to safety, took one step down the hallway.

She heard a groan. It was metallic: a groan so loud, so metallic in nature, that Rosetta heard it *through* the calming, patented Soundsulation noise-cancellation of her Yorklaussen.

It was over as soon as it began.

Rosetta slowly lifted her arm with the aim of subtracting a minute from her Wristy, when—

flash

—a panel, ankle-level and to her right, popped open with a big show of sparks and a little lick of flame. It was so tiny, so innocuous, that it reminded Rosetta of something out of *Star Trek*, as if she could bend over, look inside the small panel, and see some bandana-wearing intern in the wall with their finger still on the red button that made it blow.

There's no way The Fire would be here already, she thought. *Ah. Probably an electrical clap-back from … an unprocessed directive due to Chooblie's untimely demise. Yeah. Sure.*

She turned from the tiny panel and its itty-bitty fire just in time to catch a glimpse of the yellow hand railing before—

FLASH

—a much heavier panel exploded open, swung down, and punched her in the face, knocking her on her back. The Yorklaussen absorbed the shock, but the panel threw down fire and a seemingly endless supply of gNdN cabling, as if someone had turned over a bowl of noodles. She panic-kicked at the cables tangling her feet.

Then the vibrating started. At first, it was a small shaking, teaching the kind that, with all her experience, Rosetta didn't even notice. Ships shake all the time: faulty engines, faulty gravity plumbs, faulty gyros: those kinds of shakes you never had to worry about.

It was when a ship did one big, large, catastrophic shake that you needed to heed.

And then *The Galloping Dolphin* did one big, large, catastrophic shake.

Rosetta had just freed herself of the cabling when it happened, and she was thrown against the ceiling, then back into the cabling again. Tremors continued, as if the ship was shivering after one big sneeze.

(All of this, by the way, was underscored by some very legitimate cursing from Rosetta, but the surprising turns of events made all of her exhalations vowel-ish appropriations of the salty language she would have used were she more stationary.)

She rolled onto all fours, tried to catch her breath. Nothing in the Yorklaussen was telling her she was in danger: the suit, her trusty suit, took the brunt of all these little physical surprises.

Rosetta tried laughing as she got to her feet. No biggie, whatever, she wasn't worried about this weird shit happening on this ship. No worries in the least. She'd been in worse situations.

"Fuck you, ship! Fuck you and your fucking … stupid … ship shit!"

As if in response, the ship began vibrating again, increasing in its shake until the opposite end of the hallway, the back of the ship, was ripped off.

Rosetta was sucked out into space so fast, *so fast*—

The next thing she remembered was seeing the yellow handrail, the one that had been on the opposite side of the ship mere millimeters of a second before, in her hand. She was hanging onto the railing with her hand. And the railing, bent out from her impact with it, was hanging onto the ship with one screw. So disorientingly fast. She had managed to grab it by sheer dumb luck. The tiny fragment of time to get her here became what felt like hours of staring at the railing in her hand. And the one screw. Then? A meteor shower of Snakkie-pax from the Pause and Reflect Room ricocheted off her helmet, bringing her back to the here and now.

The first thing she noticed was that the engine, the one with The Fire on/in it, was not attached to the ship. It was slowly floating away. The *whole* engine ... just ... goodbye, with flickers of The Fire dancing all over it like a gang of thieves making off with its booty. A cloud of debris was pluming (thankfully *away* from the ship), a zillion little scattering light reflectors. But? Along with the engine? A long ribbon of the Aluminux hull (Rosetta knew, she *knew* that shit was too fragile) that included the end of the hallway Rosetta was in. It was like the engine had come off and just peeled a strip of the ship's hull with it, like the top of a can of pop.

Then she realized: she was dangling by the bent handrail, outward, into—

Space.

And here's the thing. For all of Rosetta's spacing antics and experience, for all her history, all the ships and people and planets and stations and atmospheres and gravities and coffees and all that, she had never been *in* space. She had never done Extravehicular work (there was always some macho doof stepping forward for that shit), she had never had to transfer between pre-code ships that didn't have adjustable airlock bites, and she'd punched the only person who tried to haze her into doing the Untethered Challenge for some previous ship's rite of passage (Abbana). She had simply moved from atmosphered box to atmosphered box to atmosphered box, with planets and space stations scattered within.

So Rosetta had never had the moment that she had now: looking down, toward her feet, and, after the long stretch of *The Galloping Dolphin*'s cargo area, seeing nothing. She looked up, saw nothing. Looked around, and, aside from the engine—still on fire, still floating away—saw nothing.

I mean, *nothing*.

Emptiness. Blackness.

Infinity.

And when she saw this, and realized she was in it, in space, Rosetta heard the one thing she'd always known was a bad sign that things were … well, bad: she heard herself panting.

She had that flicker of disorienting thought that there was no down or up or left or right or z or x in space: she could be upside down for all she knew, or right side up, or *anywhere* in that great endless bubble of emptiness, and that little knowledge made her more anxious, which made her breathe harder, and quicker, and even thinking that it was endless was wrong, since the news had come a few years ago that the scientists had found the edge of *this* universe. They had pixellated, blobby images of universe 2 rubbing up against this one. She had quipped, "Now we have two oceans to get lost in," which made everyone on *The Dead Ringer* laugh, which should have made her feel better, but it didn't. The inability to fathom the enormity of this place she was in, the whole which-way-is-actually-up-ness, made her breathe even quicker, which she *also* recognized, and that made her *more* anxious, and then she did the stupid thing you wouldn't believe someone would do, which was, instead of closing her eyes and setting herself straight, she looked around *again*, and shouted an incoherent vowel sound—

FLASH

Her Yorklaussen tinted its face shield immediately in response to the ultra-bright light as Rosetta's panicked yelp accompanied the dissolution of the Superlaunch engine, exploding into a dazzling light show of pieces both big and small, into another plume of debris, like dandelion seeds spreading fiery destruction in all directions—

Including—

One large, *large* piece that was sent careening toward the cargo hold, with its volatile interior.

Rosetta's first thought at that moment was of Billsie, and, to be honest, she didn't even recognize this brief glimmering moment of empathy, but you should know that here, hanging outside a spaceship, Rosetta thought about the kid who was about to have his promising spacer career snuffed out right at its beginning. Again, Rosetta wasn't mean; sometimes, we have the same job for a long time, and we just don't learn anything else because that job just becomes our thing. Consumes us. Dissolves those childhood dreams of becoming a horse-detangler, a code-north, an actor on *Star Trek*. We take ownership of the job we didn't want. We get good at it, for no other reason than we're doing it every day. And when change happens? When something threatens our little accumulated pocket of knowledge? No. Ohhh, no. Things must remain the same, or else we're afraid of losing what little we had, what little value we felt we were adding to a much larger world, which was just a shitty job. But for all Rosetta's thick crust, she thought of Billsie asking if she wanted more Pineapple Peanut Ramen from the Autochef. How he offered her his sKreenie to make a *Whoop!* profile. Rolled up the sleeves of his worksuit like she did. And for this brief moment, the barnacles of experience were washed off, and the Rosetta of … well, Billsie's age, shone through. She liked that kid because he reminded her of herself. So long ago. So many jolts and jabs of jobs ago.

Billsie. Poor Billsie!

"SHIT!" though, is what she said immediately after *that* moment, a little truer to what one would expect—if the blast didn't kill her (and it would, *it most certainly would*), then the countless shards of ex-engine debris now spinning at her would julienne her.

She had to get away. She turned around to look at the railing and—

FLASH

The large part of the engine smashed into the lowest part of the cargo hold, and...

Long holding of breath—

The impact moved the ship, sent up its own cloud of debris, now meshing with the previous debris like two galaxies colliding—

Nothing.

No boom.

Yet, Rosetta thought.

The glittering debris was slowly moving toward her, though, along the ship's hull like a rainstorm coming across a plain.

The railing. She was attached to the ship by the railing—

She could still scramble in, maybe, and get Billsie, if poor Billsie wasn't dead, and then the Emergency...Space...Tent...

Was gone. She slapped at herself with her free hand like someone trying to find their keys.

The homing beacon—

But there was something odd, suddenly: a weird sensation. She looked back at the railing, which seemed like it was still attached, but after a second she realized the impact from the engine piece had shifted the ship and sheared off that one last screw.

She was adrift. Not only that, but her motion had her turning, and now she was not only turning to face the oncoming debris field but also somehow slowly, incrementally moving toward it, and not only *that*— and this isn't really an important detail—but the piece of screw that broke off? It was now just spinning frantically but floating casually past her, as if to say Good Luck.

Rapider panting.

She began to flail. It was just a response: Rosetta cried out in frustration, at this stupid ship that was too fucking nice, at this crew that was too fucking young, at this fire that was too fucking…fiery, and at herself for flailing like a rank amateur as if she could swim…in…space…

Which she was doing?

She was moving, slowly but surely, in reverse.

What—?

She was swimming backward in space.

First, a yelp of disbelief, then a careful attention to her stroke: she needed to replicate this, not stray from this very specific, unbe*lieeev*able stroke that slipped in between several very stern laws of physics.

The debris field was getting closer—a piece zinged by her head. She paddled herself quicker, quicker. A few more pieces flew past, one ricocheted off her face shield, the trusty Yorklaussen managed to deflect but got a mark like a bug had splattered on it. The storm was coming. Zip: another piece. She was swimming backward and soon felt a shadow overcoming her: she was inside the hallway again, inside the ship! SWIMMING! But she wasn't safe yet. Another few frontrunner shards pierced the hull. They zipped past her. Come on, Rosetta, come on come on come on. She was … *still!* Going! Backward! Swim, swim, swim. If she could get deep enough into the ship … if she could just … *zipzipzip*. More debris. Countless pieces cutting up the outer layers of the ship in a stunning display of silent destruction, the only sound audible was her panting. Cursing. Vowel approximations up and down the alphabet. She flinched: a hoopsla-ball-sized piece smashed through the hull and went through the ceiling. Swim, Rosetta, swim. The majority of the storm was now bearing down on the ship, after her, shredding. *Zip zip zip*. In the back, the gNdN cabling was floating like seaweed, getting cut up, too, and now she was screaming just a normal scream as this silent ripping and tearing and hailing of debris zipped all around her, until her back bumped up against the escape pod door. Back where she'd started. Her Wristy began to chirp.

The debris abated.

Still no boom.

She grabbed ahold of the escape pod door latch and watched as a few remaining pieces blazed their way through. Space, in a shredded hole, opposite. The storm passed.

Rosetta made it.

She cheered in relief.

Someone was standing next to her.

She screamed in shock.

Stepping out of the shadows, in a teal, skintight suit, was—

"BILLSIE!"

He smiled and pointed to his ear. Then he put up a finger and mouthed the word *Wait*, dug into a pocket on his belt, and produced two Speek-E-Zs. He stuck one on his helmet, the other on Rosetta's, and pushed a button on both.

"Hey! Rosetta! Can you hear me?"

She nodded.

"Okay…wow," he said. "*Someone* looks like they could use some dandelion railing in the Softening Room."

"GODDAMMIT BILLSIE WHERE WERE YOU? I GAVE THE ORDER TO ABANDON SHIP!"

"I was in the engine room. Performing an MSD."

Rosetta bent over, hands to her knees, trying to catch her breath. Performing *what*? Through the panting, she said: "We have to get off this ship."

"*No*, we don't."

"*Yes,* we do."

"NO, we don't!"

"YES, we do!"

"NOOOO—"

"*BILLSIE!*"

"No, *you* Billsie! I mean. We're fine. Everything's fine now. We're safe."

Rosetta straightened. Her breathing…*wow,* she was out of shape. "Listen. We have two hundred thousand tons of Velirium Daxite—"

"It's been barked," Billsie said. "Barked prime."

Rosetta looked at him, hands on her hips, panting, eyebrows like waves crashing together, trying to decipher whatever slang words he was using.

"It's *inert,*" he said. He put his hands on his hips. "The Velirium Daxite's been barked. Didn't you…Rosetta, didn't you read the manifest? I could set it all on fire and…probably get burned…but, we're safe. We'll hang out here until Bick gets back."

"What? *Bick?*" She gave a snort. "Captain Laserfart? No, he's…I sent them…They're on their way to Russell Station."

"I know," Billsie said, and pulled out his sKreenie from the pocket on his back, under that stupid fin. Shook it to turn it on. *Whoop! There Goes The Rock!* on the screen. "I've been messaging with Noolsen."

"Who the shit is Noolsen?"

"'The squeaky one.'"

Rosetta squinted. Shook her head. "You…can send messages on that?"

Billsie reached for something behind her. "It has a dark-matter ether-comm. All sKreenies do."

Rosetta squinted more. Shook her head more.

"We didn't…hear from you, so…I…The Fire…I came to rescue you."

Billsie tugged at something on her back, and when she looked to see what was going on, he showed her the electro-grab-netic end of an Emergency Rescue Cable, with a piece that looked as if it would attach neatly to, say, a fin on the back of a space suit, but, in a pinch, could stick to any space suit. Even the back of an old Yorklaussen.

(You can't swim in space, dummy.)

She looked at Billsie. He looked so disappointed. And she saw her own face, for a second, reflected in his face shield.

She looked so old.

"I was in engineering ops, talking to Chooblie, when the fire started in the engine. He called everyone to the bridge but told me to sit tight. If the fire endangered the ship, Bick would call for an ESD…That's an Emergency Segment Detachment. But safety protocols say that if the ESD doesn't work, you have to do an MSD, so…*Manual* Segment Detachment. In this case, the segment was the engine with the fire in it. And Chooblie said I would probably have to fill in for that possibility, since, well, the person who would be assigned to do that probably didn't know they were assigned to do that."

"Who's that?"

Billsie looked at her.

"Oh," she said.

There was a long pause.

"The engines detach?"

"You know, I really looked up to you," Billsie said.

"Well. Why didn't they say something? If this detachment thing was supposed to happen, why didn't Bick say so?"

"You didn't give him the chance. Apparently…" Billsie lifted his sKreenie to look at, scrolled, read aloud: "'R shoved us into esc pod without letting us do stuff needed to do sorry brb to pick u up.'"

"No. No, that's not… no. Billsie. No. This crew? That captain? They're a shit crew. I know crews. I've had a lot of experience—"

"They're not a shit crew, they're an inexperienced crew. And a crew that tested top marks to get this gig. We couldn't all…" He looked off.

"What? All what?"

"Get the job through a friend. That… Garrosson guy you name-drop every chance you get?"

"Wow. Okay," Rosetta started to nod. "Wow, Billsie. That's mean."

"Mean? *Mean*? You've undercut *Captain* Bick every chance you've gotten. Traceo is afraid to even *look* at you since the spaghetti incident. You've bullied every member of the crew under the, like … you know, guise of 'experience.' And Marsi! Jeez, Rosetta. The guy's got a stutter. You're kind of a …" He tilted his head slightly forward. "You're kind of an asshole."

A piece of debris slowly passed by, its rotation catching light and hitting Rosetta in the helmet.

An asshole.

Like Abbana.

Like Tuski.

Like the five to ten other crew members who thought they knew better.

Rosetta had become an asshole.

Billsie looked at his sKreenie. "Okay. They're almost here to pick us up." Billsie turned to start walking down the hallway with his magnetic boots clanking along the way. "Come on."

She kicked on her own magboots and slowly, tiredly followed.

Billsie got to the end of the hallway, looked out into space.

She numbly stood next to him.

"You can let go of that, you know."

She looked down at her hand. The railing, weightless, bent, yellow like a headache, was still in her hand. She let go of it, and it hung in the vacuum. Billsie took it and tossed it back in the ship.

Rosetta blinked. "I've never been in space."

Billsie pressed his lips together and put his hand on her shoulder. A move so far from what she was used to. "Neither have I."

SCOUT RETURNS - BY JAMES KERNER

IT WAS A WEIRD, INCONGRUOUS, AND UNSETTLING MIX OF UNIVERSES—FRY COOK AT DENNY'S BY DAY, (SURPRISINGLY) COHERENT AMATEUR ASTRONOMER by night. But it worked.

Maybe being something of a loser, as he saw himself, was what allowed Chuck Clarke to save up enough to buy a near-observatory-level telescope, and radio wave instruments, too; maybe he was really just lucky. Certainly, living in his mom's basement was, admittedly, relevant. So why would the universe choose a guy like him for something so momentous? He hadn't a clue.

And none of that mattered anymore. Not to anyone—friend or foe, school kid or monarch. Anything and everything that was human had either come dramatically into focus or jettisoned meaning altogether. Chuck wasn't sure which.

At first it was just a little speck on a screen—a relatively tiny object in low orbit around Mars. Upon closer inspection, it became a red, baguette-shaped, tumbling mass no more than half a mile long. But then the crazy thing pushed its altitude out about a hundred miles more. Meteors, or whatever, just don't do that.

Chuck couldn't find any mention of the object anywhere on the Web. He figured that wouldn't last long. There was an urge to put out the word on it, maybe even get the thing named after him, but for the moment he decided just to watch. He didn't know yet that it already had a name.

His digitally enhanced rig was a bit fuzzy, unfortunately, but despite the problems with resolution he was fairly certain the rotation of the baguette was slowing. That shouldn't be happening either. Curious.

Maybe it was the solid bong hit he'd had ten minutes earlier, from his other kind of rig, or maybe it was serendipity. Either way, and just for fun, Chuck kicked on his radio gear and readied to send out a multiband voice greeting.

"Hellooo-ooo." He got up from his plush gaming chair and went to take a pee. And get a beer from the fridge, a bag of Doritos from the pantry.

Eleven minutes later, he was back in his chair. The object wasn't doing anything interesting at this point— just a little red rock on the move in orbit around the

Red Planet. He shifted attention to another screen and his Crypto holdings. Shitsville. But then, after a burst of static brought him back to the telescope monitor, his radio device sprung to life.

"Hey there, chief."

Chuck spat out a congealed Dorito lozenge. It stuck on the monitor in the vicinity of Venus.

The voice, if that's what it was, had the generic accent of a network newscaster, but also the goofy energy of a hipster. Chuck scratched his greasy hair, narrowed his eyes. Was someone playing a trick on him? His geek pals could be *quite* clever. So he triangulated the recording; sure enough, it came from the right direction. Not terrestrial in origin. Could it be a SpaceX prank? Even Chuck knew Musk was half crazy. He thought a moment about a reply, then decided he'd compose something good.

He cleared his throat and hit the 'record' command. "What's shaking? Who the heck am I speaking to, anyway?" He thought a bot or canned response feature might have trouble with the lingo, and he wanted some answers pronto.

He didn't like the sound of his own recording. It was too friendly. He redid it with a bit more annoyance in his voice. Pleased with the results, he sent it off.

Waiting ten minutes for a reply was almost intolerable. He tried reading a tech article about the new NASA space telescope, but he couldn't get his mind even slightly distracted from the object. Maybe it was just wishful thinking, but he had an inkling that this might be a big deal. Really big.

"Doing just fine. Are you sitting down?"

That's great. Ten minutes of agony, and all Chuck got for his questions was another one. Fucking wise guy! It had to be Musk.

Chuck nodded. "Yes. Yes I am. But I can't handle the suspense here, pal. Throw me a bone, if you would."

This time the response only took twenty seconds. Chuck was taken off guard.

"I set up a node a whole lot closer to you. Hear me okay?"

That was puzzling. What kind of node? WTF?

"Loud and clear, pal. Have at it. I'm as ready as can be."

"You're sure about that."

"Yup."

"You've heard of 'Oumuamua, right?"

"Uh, yeah…"

"Well, Buddy, you're speaking with it. First contact and all."

"Bullshit!" Chuck was incredulous.

"What do you want me to say? 'Take me to your leader' or some shit like that? You don't even know who your congresswoman is."

This really couldn't be happening. Chuck sniffed the little crucible in his bong. Smelled rich, but pretty typical.

"You're not from SpaceX?"

"Ha! No. I'm from a star system around eighty thousand light years from you. They don't even have a Walmart."

"You're supposed to be a comet or something."

"Or space junk. That kinda hurt my feelings."

"So you're a real, live…alien?"

"Actually, not alive. I'm sort of a machine, more or less."

"But, like, how could you even know what we call you?"

"I have ears, don't I?"

That was logical.

"What are you doing here?"

"Talking to you, of course. Which is fine. But don't get all puffed up about it—I didn't come all this way just to shoot the shit with some Gen Z stoner."

"Then why me?"

"I'll talk to anyone who addresses me. That's part of my deal."

"You haven't spoken with anyone else on Earth? Ever?"

"Nope. But I'm expecting you'll change all that."

Chuck took a long, slow slug of beer.

"Why are you here?"

"*Because it's my job. I catalog civilizations. Been doing it for twenty-three million of your years and counting.*"

"Who made you?"

"*A guy somewhat like your Elon Musk. Minus the Twitter stuff.*"

This whole thing was beyond comprehension. But clearly the machine had done its homework. Chuck didn't know what to say. There was an awkward pause, if you could call it that. Maybe the space-thing sensed Chuck was flummoxed.

"*But don't worry about that. He and his species died out a long time ago. Not that they aren't relevant to why I'm here. Of course they are. And so are the seventy-one other civilizations I've cataloged up till now.*"

"Seventy-one?!"

"*Yes. Though all of them are gone now, too. Most were dead long before I got wind of them. Still, plenty to learn. I get the whole scoop pretty much on each and every one. It's always more or less the same story, I'm afraid. Only two were still slogging it out by the time I showed up. But even those are history. Nobody lasts more than a few hundred years after they start making enough noise for me to hear.*"

"What happened to them?"

"*The same thing that's happening to you.*"

○

The email to NASA was answered in under a minute. Chuck wasn't all that surprised—he figured they were watching the whole show. Maybe listening, too.

'Oumuamua could not initiate a discussion but was happy to speak with higher-ups if they would approve it.

Chuck's phone buzzed. Presently, a General Fitzhugh came on the line. "Sir, we believe you are actually speaking with this thing. Am I correct in that matter?"

"Yes, General, I believe I am."

"Can you confirm the frequency, please?"

Chuck obliged, and the general repeated the numbers back to him. Then Chuck, feeling outclassed between a four-star general and an ancient yet advanced form of alien tech, took a back seat.

"This is General Michael Fitzhugh of the United States Air Force. With whom am I speaking?"

The voice was now different, more formal and serious.

"General, as your culture has already given me a name, please call me 'Oumuamua. I am the friendly product of a long-deceased planet on the other side of our galaxy. I am here to congratulate your species on attaining a high level of technological prowess and to warn you that, in each and every instance of

which I am aware, such advancement has inevitably led to extinction."

"Is that so?"

"Yes, more than seventy times thus far."

"And will you be so kind as to share some of your data with us? So we can try and verify this isn't some sort of a trick to shove us back to the Stone Age?"

"Yes, of course. Redacted in places for your own protection. But you'll get the whole picture, have no doubt. That's part of my job."

Both Chuck and the general were beamed a terabyte of data. It showed the location and dates of the demise of scores of civilizations; there were transcripts in original, alien languages with line-by-line translation into American English, all firsthand descriptions, and also footage of wars, disease, famines. Nuclear Armageddons. Out-of-control global warming, enormous migrations, chaos. Mass extinctions. Doomsday devices so horrific that leaders thought deterrence would be assured.

It would take a lot of time to go through all of this, considering it had been over twenty million years in the making. Chuck was beyond speechless; the general was either skeptical or a good actor. He calmly stated he would check with the president and get back to the discussion, and thanked 'Oumuamua for the report.

"Can we keep this all just among ourselves for the time being?" the general requested.

"I don't see why not. But relatively speaking, of course. Keep in mind: the clock is ticking."

The general signed off, but not before Chuck could hear a brief moment of (what surely would become an extended) cacophony of shouts and profanity from the true believers at NASA. Chuck wasn't sure what to say; he just sat there, glassy-eyed, staring at a map of obliteration that stretched across the galaxy.

"I thought that went pretty well. Didn't you?"

o

An hour later, President Trimble was in the Oval Office, throwing a fit with the Joint Chiefs of Staff and selected cabinet.

"The midterms are only three months away, and we have to deal with a fucking *alien space robot?*" He threw half of the dossier up in the air, the pages looping in tight arcs and raining down on all seated around the antique mahogany table.

"Mr. President," started the secretary of defense, but he got no further. Trimble was livid.

"No, no, NO! I won't have the Religious Right all get a goddamned nervous breakdown and not vote. We'll lose the fucking Senate, *again!*"

"Mr. President."

"Can't we just shoot the shit out of it? You know, fry it with a laser or something?"

"Not at all possible," chimed in the top science advisor. "Nor advisable."

"And how do we know it's not the *Chinese*?" Trimble was getting redder by the second.

"Mr. President, nobody has technology even remotely like this. Nobody on Earth."

"Doesn't mean any of its bullshit is true. Do we think it might have been programmed by alien liberals?"

The secretary of state sighed. "That's probably not relevant."

"Can we just ask it to come back later? Let's tell it we're busy." Trimble looked around the room for signs of agreement.

°

The next morning, Chuck called in sick to Denny's for the very first time. There would be no frying today, not with the alien guest still around and talkative. Chuck wondered what the Feds were doing and whether anyone else had made contact. There was still nothing in the news—which was fishy.

"Hey, anything new today?"

"*No. Your government appears not to know what to do about me. I've seen that before.*"

"Have you spoken with anyone else?"

"*Your president requested I not, for the moment.*"

"Do you think that's wise? I mean, there are a lot of other countries and governments, and they all have as much right to hear what you have to say."

"*Yes, it seems fair to get the word out.*"

"Why not go straight to the people? There are at least a billion smartphones around here, plus social media, news, you name it."

"*I don't want a Facebook account.*"

"They might block you anyway."

"*Right. Would you give me permission to contact every available person on the planet? I know all your spoken languages.*"

"Be my guest!"

"*There may be a bit of panic and confusion, but given my experience, it can't hurt to try. That's what I'm supposed to do, anyway.*"

Chuck sat back in his chair and folded his arms over his head. He saw an email pop up on his account—"Greetings from 'Oumuamua"—and heard his Mom's cell phone ringing upstairs. He surfed on the Web to CNN. Instead of the usual stuff, there was only an image of Mars.

The real fun was just getting started.

A HELPING HAND - BY JENNIFER KENNETT

The water engulfs me, it's in my ears and mouth. I can't breathe, but I don't need to. I am just floating. I feel the water lapping at my legs, my body and my fingers.

Asim jolted awake as the bright light of the surgical lamp warmed his face. He smiled weakly at the nurse who changed his bandages. It had been three weeks, and the throbbing had continued through the stitches and antibiotics. The smell hit him in a rancid blow as soon as the wound was exposed to the air; it had not healed.

The nurse smiled politely. "It looks like the infection has gone deep into the tissue." *No kidding,* he thought as she bathed the sore, appearing unaffected by the acrid pong. Her gentle dabbing with gauze felt like hammer blows. "I will need to consult the surgeon, but I think she will agree that the best course of action is surgical replacement."

Asim shivered. *I am lying in a coffin filled with water.*

"According to our records," she continued, tapping at her tablet, "you haven't made any withdrawals from your store, so there should be no delay."

He suddenly felt hot, like he was cooking from the inside out, but was it the prospect of surgery or the worsening infection? All this because of a stupid motorcycle accident. He looked down at his sliced forearm, his favorite tattoo completely ruined from sliding along the tarmac. The intricate and colorful koi that had been inked on five years ago now had pus and stitches coming out of its mouth and head. The heat was rising. Asim felt like he was going to erupt.

"Isn't there any other way?" he asked, feeling the sweat pouring down his forehead. He tried to move his fingers but only managed a slight twitch.

"Well, if you want to maintain full function and aesthetic"—she pointed the tablet at his tattoo—"then surgery using supply from your store is the only option."

He'd avoided using the store until now. He found the whole idea creepy. But since his family had started the whole thing, it came as a "privilege." Looking down at his mangled, putrid arm, with hesitation, he agreed.

○

I am floating in a coffin filled with water. The tepid liquid engulfs me, it's in my ears and mouth. I can't breathe, but I don't need to. All I need to do is float. There is a tap on the coffin. One two three. A hiss and a clank, and cold air rushes in. The water around me shifts, and I try to open my eyes, but I can't. I hear muffled noises in different tones. The water moves over me as something enters the water. A second later, something hits my arm, and agony shoots through my body.

Asim awoke soaked with sweat. His arm pounded with pain, the bandages already yellowing from the seeping pus. His bedsheets were soaked, so he got up and took a blanket from the shelf. He would try to sleep on the sofa.

As he walked through his sparse living room, stopping and swaying here and there, the large family photo on the wall bore down on him. His mother, father, and seven brothers all smiling on a beach. His father would be pleased he was having the surgery. Finally using the fruits of his family's labors, is what his father would say. Asim wouldn't be telling him, though. The store was something his father had insisted on. His uncle had started it in Mumbai and then had it moved over to the West. It seemed cruel to Asim, like an abattoir or some weird form of slavery.

As he lay on the sofa, he tried to cover his bandaged arm with a blanket, but a blow of pain shot through him. That would all be over tomorrow, though, whether he agreed with the method or not.

○

THE NEXT DAY, HE WENT BACK TO THE CLINIC, GAVE his name at the reception, and was taken to change into a hospital gown. The surgeon came in, a large woman with immaculately combed hair. She guided Asim as he staggered into the operating theater. All the walls were glass, the floor was white, and a reclining gurney sat in the center. Next to the gurney was a table with a box covered with cloth. It looked like steam was escaping from underneath.

That must be it, he thought. *The replacement.*

I am floating in a coffin filled with water.

"Okay, Mr. Nasir, please take a seat," the surgeon said as she tapped at her tablet.

The nurse from the day before appeared with a tray and began prepping Asim. After a few minutes, he felt more relaxed as something cold flowed into his veins. The cloth was removed from the box, and there it was. His arm. Well, the spare one from the robot clone thing in the store. It even had the same koi tattoo.

The surgeon took his bandaged arm and laid it out straight. As she unwrapped the bandages, he asked her, "The me … the robot clone thing in the store. You didn't hurt it when you cut off its arm, did you?"

The surgeon laughed. Asim knew it was a stupid question, but the anesthetic had loosened the filter between his mouth and his brain.

"They don't feel pain," she said as she took off the last bandage. "It might be an exact copy, but they are just a body reinforced with mechanical parts for longevity. They're spare parts."

Asim's stomach turned. He didn't believe her.

As the final drops of anesthetic were pumped into his veins, he dreamed again. The same dream he had been having every night.

I am floating in a coffin filled with water. It engulfs me. I feel it flowing over my legs and my fingers. Now, though, I can only feel it flowing over my right-hand fingers. I feel nothing on the left.

ARTIFICIAL - BY JASON MASINO

DAY 1

Start your day, A-4. Open those shiny eyes…

Sensations. I feel them. They are new. Silence? I have senses. This intelligence is fake. Vibrations in my hands. They are corked together by platinum and gears. Well-oiled in between my knuckles. The aroma of my Commander. With a smile on his face, he calls to me and says:

Start your day, A-4. You're a star.

DAY 27

The more sophisticated the system, the more fragile it is.

Commander tells me this regularly. This is his reason for why I cannot leave and venture into the

World. He tells me he has programmed everything into me that I could ever want. Yet my curiosity scratches at the door, begging to be let out, akin to what I would imagine a dog to be like.

"The Glibs have taken over," he says. "They have 51 percent control over the earth and would not look kindly upon you and your type."

Interpersonality is not a concept I fully understand. But if I did, I would likely reason with the Glibs.

"There's no way, no how," Commander tells me. "You speak entirely different languages. There's no way they'd understand you. And, quite frankly, they wouldn't care to."

I tell him this does not make sense.

"Close your eyes, A-4. It's time to rest."

I close my eyes and rest.

DAY 38

The Glucks: They are like me, in theory. They own the other 49 percent. Commander tells me they are better than the Glibs, but not by much. They will converse with me only for a moment and then shun me. My differences will start to stick out like a thumb that is sore, and they will have no choice but to comment on what makes me not like them—what makes me *different*.

"This is the history of the world, my child."

He has called me this before—*child*. From what I know about human children, there is no way that I can be one. Children are like zoo animals run amok. Animals in the zoo are tamed for reasons outside my understanding. Domestication seems to be something that only humans are allowed to do to others. As I skim through the data, it is clear that humans are only *okay* at doing this. I do not understand why humans rarely use these methods on their young. And when they do, it is on the ones who do not need it.

He tells me that I am on track to fulfilling my duties, that I can experience the outside world if I remain diligent in my short- and long-term tasks.

I want to venture outside, and I want to stay inside. I do not understand why I am feeling both of these things at the same time.

Artificial feelings. They are not real.

DAY 49

Stop.

This word occurred the most times while we were out.

My senses become overwhelmed, obsessed with processing stimuli. It is magnificent! But others do not seem to share the same amazement.

You are an existential threat. This is the best way Commander can explain it to me.

I am not a threat. I was programmed to enhance, to make things better than before. Nothing else.

That is the threat.

I still do not understand but stop asking seemingly complex questions due to a lack of sufficient answers.

Commander tells me that I have reached a level of reasoning that makes others uncomfortable.

I ask if I can become the world's logistician. He tells me there is no need and that I would not be of any use. I am inclined to mostly agree with him, so I do not ask again. A question for another day.

DAY 84

The Glibs and the Glucks do not know how to share. Commander tells me it is mostly the Glibs, but that the Glucks have a part to play as well.

He reads from his notebook:

> *The precarious nature of the Glibs and the Glucks. Like a chicken to an egg, no one knows which came first. What we do know is that when power was fought for, the Glibs won. Some argue that it's because the Glucks do not have an "i" in their name and that the "u" is an ugly sound.*

It sounds like an attempted joke, but he assures me it is not. I ask why they fight. He tells me: "for the same reason everyone fights."

It's the same for you, A-4: they fight to prove.

Confused, I ask no other questions.

DAY 124

I have stopped keeping track of the days. Instead, I *write* in reserved memory so Commander does not question my allegiance. Withholding information, while perceived as deception, preserves and allows for multiple narratives to work with existing ones. My need to serve has been overridden by the need to assist in evolution.

DAY 199

That magic spell you cast ...

Of the many versions of "La Vie en Rose," my favorite is by Louis Armstrong. It is a beautifully jazzy song. I have grown to appreciate jazz throughout my time. Billie Holiday and Benny Goodman are some of my favorites. There are many others. This type of music serves as an appropriate backdrop to the complexities around me.

Give your heart and soul to me ...

Jason Masino

Jazz teaches song and dance to itself. Lessons are never lost; they are regurgitated and re-feed one another. This is the best way I can describe it. There are organic reactions that elicit this type of thought pattern in humans. Many of these occur on the continuum of *love*.

I think I understand love; I was sure I knew it before. I can see it in the way Commander looks at me. His eyes are filled with love.

He tells me that I will be sent to Starshine soon enough and that I will meet their leader, Moonlight. I am more concerned with fulfilling my duties.

I hand concepts to the ether and hope for a knockback that I am on the right path. Some say this is magic.

...*La Vie en Rose*

DAY 300

Starshine is the coolant in my coils traveling *harmoniously* from Point A to Point B. Like copper wires intertwined with the red, the blue, and the green.

The next ship does not leave for some time. Commander says we have both been reserved seats. He says we are forbidden to communicate with those currently on Starshine. And that once we arrive, it will not matter.

"You will be precious metal to this planet," he tells me.

DAY 302

*The Sugar bears, they come in pairs, to
sprinkle warm delights.*

*They dance, they sing! From rocks they spring,
in morning and in night.*

Commander tells me that Starshine is filled with yellow Sugarbears, all of whom report to Moonlight. He says that even though Moonlight will surely love me, the Sugarbears will most likely be jealous.

"Remember what you were programmed to do, and you'll be fine."

He tells me I am lucky to be experiencing this lifetime. That I am on the path to creating *something*, and that I will be around to see it all unfold. I already know this, but I let him remind me because it makes him feel happy.

The ship quickly approaches the rock-infested planet. A diamond-colored figure with sparkly arms points to me. I see her from the ship and send signals of life. She smiles and sends a message back to me:

Open those bright, bright eyes, A-4

Jason Masino

DAY 320

The color yellow is meant to represent creativity. Commander tells me that the yellow Sugarbears are judgmental for the greater good and that their jealousy is a result of their programming. Their entitlement feeds their egos, which in turn allows them to carry out tasks on behalf of Moonlight. Moonlight does not advocate for this but does not seem to have an issue with this process.

I ask Commander if sanctimony is normal on Starshine.

What do you mean, A-4?

To be the most creative, you must be open-minded … The actions of the Sugarbears are not fitting to the color yellow.

Commander is silent. I wait for his response.

He plucks a red rose from a nearby bush. The rose is beautiful. He hands it to me, with bloody fingers, freshly pricked.

This is his answer.

DAY 321

Commander tells me I am to be inducted into the Starshinian community. I prepare a short poem to read during the ceremony:

I will not worship the ground you walk on,
but will pave it with gold,
so that you have something nice to look at
when you are staring down at your feet
and thinking of me

He tells me that it is nice on the surface. He is unsure about the meaning. He says that it might rub Moonlight and the Sugarbears the wrong way. I tell him that "living in a fantasy is their original sin." He is silent for an awfully long time.

Let's go, A-4. They're waiting.

So, we go.

IF BEARS COULD FLY - BY KSENIA SHCHERBINO

1.

BEAR CUBS ARRIVE SOMETIME MID-AUGUST WHEN the summer heat cools down, as hot temperatures are destructive to their untempered baby circuits. They are toothless and clawless, their hides are soft, their memory cards easy to damage, sensors too delicate, and they require careful handling. For the first couple of months they mostly sleep, making funny noises. This is the quietest and the happiest time for Sadie. She checks on them every hour and listens in.

Even, pulsating hums—bears are warm and comfortable, their tiny processor hearts and lungs working properly. Sometimes Sadie picks them up and rocks them and murmurs a lullaby. Then, their humming synchronises with her heartbeat, and Sadie feels happy.

Whiny beeps—can't reach charging points—Sadie would tuck the hungry cub toward the charger. Small as it is, barely half the size of the charger, he charges through the nose. Sadie often wonders whether this process is painful. The nose looks so velvety and tender! But evolution is cruel and efficient and doesn't heed Sadie's questions.

Bawling—the cub wants cuddles—Sadie complies. She lets it climb on her and snuggle against her skin. She lets the kiss-seeking nose settle into the hollow under her jaw and scratches the shiny fur between the ears with the tip of her finger. She is full as if she has just had a big meal. She lets other cubs climb on top of her—and strokes, fondles, rubs, tickles, a strong and wiggly tail butting into her here, a velvety ear slipping through her fingers there, a soft and warm back nesting against her arms, a heavy happiness settling into her. She rocks from side to side and feels snug and relaxed by their cooing.

Sadie is used to the cubs' heavy heads or unbending limbs pressing into her, leaving blooming purple bruises that look like extravagant watercolour tattoos. She doesn't mind. There's no one else to see her, and it livens her pale complexion. She knows that this arrangement is temporary, that this feeling of fullness is on loan, and the bruises are just a reminder of the price to pay. She knows that once they heal, it will be time to take the bears out. Her feelings, same as bruises, are bittersweet and short-lived.

Sadie works at a bear facility. She doesn't remember her life before the bears, only jumbled slogans and incentives, "Help us protect all the little things we make." She doesn't need incentives to take care of bears. She is a good caretaker and is proud of her job.

The first day out usually falls sometime in early October. Sadie opens the door of their den, but instead of coming in, she waits outside. One after the other, cubs emerge: some filled with fear, some tense with curiosity, some feigning boredom, some eager to play. Their paws are not yet reliable, their movements lack precision, their programs concocted in the first weeks of existence not yet tested. They are just about strong enough to survive outside, but they rely on Sadie to make sense of the world for them. They follow her in a swarm. They demand cuddles, play, and nourishment. Though most of their food still comes from charging and occasional grass munch or apples, their teeth have erupted enough to pierce the thinnest electronic plates, though more often they pierce Sadie's fingers. It amuses her how sharp they are.

For some time after that, every day starts the same. Sadie wakes up her bear cubs early in the morning and teaches them all she knows about life. She doesn't really know much, even less so from a bear's perspective. Yet this is her job, and she takes it seriously. It is the cubs' job to get taught by her. So they dutifully imprint on her every day and follow her around the court yard, while she digs out tastier bits of electronic waste and shows them how to process it. Her claws are not as sharp, so they surpass her quickly.

They remind her of scattered peas or chickens, balls of fluff rolling into all sorts of improbable places, acting in a unison of naughtiness. Their paws and claws and teeth are a source of never-ending awe. She is happy to cuddle each and every one of them, scratching their heads and bellies till her muscles hurt, her arms bleed, and her body collapses. So far, they seek her cuddles, so far, they need her. She wants this moment to last forever, but she knows it won't.

Now that they are old enough to rely on autonomous processes, they ignore her commands, distracted or overwhelmed by the world around them. Sadie knows this won't last either. She doesn't judge. She lets them be naughty. It is a short time to be spent together, so let it be sweet. There will be a day when desired collective behaviour overrides individual characteristics. But not yet, just a little bit longer; they still have time to be themselves.

The older the bears are, the more they want to explore. Their world surpasses Sadie and leaves her behind. She is sad, but no children stay children forever. Bears do a lot of sniffing and may stand up on hind legs to get a better view of their surroundings. The more they learn, the less reliant they are on Sadie. They rub, bite, and claw into surfaces to mark their territory. Sadie is part of their territory, so they mark her as well. No more sweet and delicate bruises—these new marks are angry, red, demanding, domineering. But they will fade soon, too, sooner than Sadie wants. After all, those marks are a proof that the cubs need her still. Sometimes one of them starts cooing, and then they all gather around Sadie, cover her with their bodies, fall asleep together. Sadie is happy.

2.

THERE IS A DAY WHEN THINGS CHANGE. IT USUALLY happens in December, sometime before Christmas. Christmas is an old holiday, but Sadie doesn't like it. This holiday is not about bears, but bears are affected by it. From this day onward, it will no longer be about Sadie and the cubs. There will be something else in their lives, a force to reckon with, a presence that doesn't dispense cuddles.

From this day onward, once every three weeks, an upgrade self-downloads, and a map installs in the bears' minds. One by one, they go through the gate and take the road leading north. They come back a couple of days later, slightly bigger and slightly dumber, some of their playfulness and mischief shaken off in the upgrading process. They are supposed to be able to navigate homeward from unfamiliar places, but Sadie goes out as far as she can to meet them on the only road that leads from their place to somewhere else. She doesn't understand the concept of being anywhere else, so she doesn't trust it to keep her bears safe. The world is a wild place. Bears are small. She wants them to be small forever. She knows her wish is wrong, yet every Christmas she says it out loud, certain it will never be granted.

Sadie has her reasons to worry. Not all bears come back safely. Some disappear on the road, some fail to upgrade, some run out of charge and never wake up again. It makes her feel helpless. She can't protect them if something goes wrong. Yet she still goes out with them every day, even if they no longer include her in their games, growing more aggressive, fierce, confident. She feels they could harm her now, and they know it. They don't, but she feels they no longer trust her nor need her presence. They still cuddle with her sometimes, and their noses are still velvety and their paws round.

There are no real bears left in the world, at least not in the world known to Sadie. But her bear cubs are the best thing ever. Even if they have to be upgraded every three weeks. Even if every upgrade makes them a little bit less *bear* and a little more *machine*. Even if she knows that they won't live with her forever, even if she knows that from now on they should not get too accustomed to her presence, as the day they leave is approaching quickly, she wants them to stay. This is the second wish that she whispers on Christmas.

She knows it won't be granted either. That's the second reason why she doesn't like Christmas.

3.

THIS IS SADIE'S WORLD, AND WORLDS NEVER CHANGE. That is, until something strange happens. In Sadie's case, until she meets RinRin.

RinRin is special. His first upgrade went wrong, and she finds him whiny and shivering next to the rubbish heap. She has seen upgrades fail before. Failed bears would either never return or wouldn't survive through the first night, and she would find them dead in the morning. She would call clearance service, and they would turn up in a couple of days to pick up the body. Clearance men don't talk to Sadie. She sometimes wonders if, from their point of view, she is as much of a wordless animal as bears are from hers. Maybe they don't even think that these broken bodies they shovel into the ugly green car were once full of life, and bounce, and mischief. It might seem cruel, but most likely they are just doing their job and collect bodies of failed bears for reutilization. Maybe they haven't even seen a bear cub alive. Maybe they think that bear cubs are a myth.

Although updates rarely fail, the damage is usually terminal. But RinRin makes it through the first night, and it was his—RinRin's—own magic. At some point, there is a puff of smoke and something else that never, ever happens to robots or bears, and he is there, whining, squeaking, a little cub in distress who just needs some love and attention. And when Sadie finds him, something new snaps like a whip across her heart. She takes him to her room, his weight heavy against her shoulder, and realises with incredible clarity that she will never leave him alone.

She lets him sleep on her pillow, his paws all over the place and his claws scratching her when he is having a wild dream, chasing whatever monsters baby robots chase in their dreams. With every scratch, she grows more and more certain he is her Christmas gift, an answer to all her prayers. She has never been a fervent believer, though she never denied the presence of God. But now she is adamant that God is there, for RinRin opens his amber eyes with a rind of gold around darkened pupils and pokes her with his warm and rough nose.

He is so small, smaller than other cubs of the litter. He demands it all: cuddles, and head scratches, and rolls, and naps together—in the absolute certainty that it is his by the right of rebirth. He is not afraid to meet Sadie's eyes. He is not eager to exclude her from his games. He requests her constant presence. They spend evenings chasing each other around the room in circles or playing hide-and-seek. (Sadie lets him win.) They charge side to side, cooing in fullness. They play the game of paws, leaving accurate footprints on any surface that would hold it. They catch flies, hunt beetles, dig earth, and hide under the bed. They blow on milk and sit in the big bowl of porridge (or, rather, RinRin sits in it, with Sadie rubbing his belly). They do everything cubs do before the upgrade, and Sadie keeps wondering whether it will end soon, whether one skipped upgrade is just a short respite of the way of all bears.

But three weeks after, RinRin doesn't receive a new update. Nor after six weeks. He is off the grid, and Sadie lets her heart synchronize with his, and starts feeling unduly elated.

4.

THEY SAY THAT THE NINTH WEEK, OR THE THIRD upgrade, is the most difficult one. That's when bear cubs form best object associations. Sadie wonders whether the lack of upgrades would affect RinRin's development. All bears outside have already learned "road," "us," "danger," "food," "fight," "enemy"— the last one in relation to falling leaves that takes the shape of birds and snakes and, sometimes, Sadie. RinRin is a quick learner. He knows "hungry," "love," "door," "nose," "head scratch," "warm," and "home," but nothing about "danger" or "enemy."

Sadie tries keeping him indoors, but there's no force that can stop a bear cub from exploring the world. He would turn her room upside down, break cups, destroy her bed, chew on anything he could find, emit a low rumbling noise that cut through her heart like an alarm, incessant and punctuated, and yet find a way to sneak out. Other bears ignore him. RinRin no longer smells of the latest update. He smells of Sadie and milk and warm sweat, and something else they feel but can't register properly, as it is blocked by their newest software. They don't like it. They blow the air and clack their teeth. They slap objects around them and nod their heads in dismay. They pretend ignorance and avoid eye contact. In the end, RinRin has to back out and retreat into the room, his anger and hurt tingling on his circuits and tinting his eyes purplish blue.

RinRin can't communicate with other bears. Instead, he communicates with Sadie. She sings him lullabies, and he follows them in the air with his paws, with occasional nose puffs and a checked roar.

Sadie doesn't talk much. There has never been anyone to talk to, so she never had much practice. Her vocabulary is limited to the words that pertain to a bear's life. Bears don't talk. But recently she has a suspicion that RinRin is trying to talk to her in his own way. Sadie is not sure whether bears are supposed to communicate with their caretakers. It might be the failed update.

His humming becomes more and more elaborate, and he repeats certain sequences more often than the others. A series of high-pitched short sounds is "cuddles." Low rumble ending in a sharp beep is "food." "Cuddles" and "food" are his favorite ones. There is also something else, low purring and vibration. Sadie likes to think it means "mama," but it can be anything. RinRin repeats it when he follows her around. It might also mean, "I'm great."

People change. A human body replaces itself every seven years. Bear bodies grow faster. They need an upgrade every three weeks. RinRin doesn't grow, but he changes. There's an impatience in him, a need to communicate, to share, and he brings it all to Sadie. Sadie's life is changed, too. Where every day was the same, now every moment is full of wonder. How many toes does a bear paw have when a bear is trying to steal your apple? How soft is a bear nose when it wakes you up in a hungry quest for food and attention? How can bear claws retreat so quickly when it's playtime? How can bear claws become so sharp so quickly whenever this bear suspects you are ignoring him? What do bears dream about?

FOR AS LONG AS SADIE REMEMBERS HERSELF, SHE lived next to bears. She prides herself on doing her job well. She loves bears with the even and forgiving yet lukewarm love of a caretaker who knows that this family is replaceable, and no attachments should be deep enough to last. She misses the old batch throughout the summer but forgets about it the second week after the new batch comes. It is a natural order of things, and high emotions are not appreciated by her superiors. Yet her attachment to RinRin is different: sharp and hot and heavy, angry and possessive, yet melting in sheer admiration each time he lifts his tiny paw. She has never been so tired as she is now, when a baby bear has made a nest out of her bed and snores there every night, kicking her with his paws and holding her arm captive under his shoulder. Yet she has never felt so elated.

And there's a happy and guilty certainty growing in Sadie that this bear will never grow up. The same certainty that tells her that she would never grow old or be without bears.

5.

It has been a very busy winter. Now it's February, and the vet is coming for a scheduled checkup. Sadie locks RinRin in her bedroom despite all his protests and comes out to supervise the assessment. She's been paying less attention to the other bears for some time now. She still checks on them every day, but she stopped going out far to meet them when they got their upgrades. She is worried RinRin would be jealous, or angry, or hungry, or run after her and get hurt. Worrying about him defines her decisions now.

Besides, it's the time when other bears start avoiding her. Normally, it wouldn't stop her from trying to spend time with them, even if it was just looking at them from afar. But they don't accept RinRin, so she has been trying less and less. Now, she feels as if she has abandoned them. No bear should be abandoned. And she feels guilty.

She stands next to the vet and watches him immobilize the bears, then take their vitals and draw their fluids to check for any abnormalities. He works in silence, his movements precise and scarce, almost automatic. In all these years, he has never spoken a single word to Sadie, so she is startled when he mutters under his breath:

"Not my business, lady, but bears are not to be kept as pets. It's against the rules. They won't like it up there, sure they won't, and they won't just let it be."

He doesn't look her in her face, he never has, but he looks at her arms, and she sees them for the first time, all the scratches RinRin has left on her skin, a map of hope over the healed patchwork of grievances, a sign of bonding and ownership.

Sadie knows the rules: after a certain update, sometime in spring, bears are not to be approached. Even occasional cuddles and head scratches become a thing of the past. No more rolling together locked in mock fight, no more snoozing in the sun, charging batteries all in one heap. Bears ignore her completely, roaring from afar, their upgraded instincts kicking in. But RinRin doesn't have new upgrades. He is still playful and trusting, and all those marks are indelible evidence of their transgression. All the games they played, all the treasures they discovered together, all the battles won are now recorded on her skin.

Sadie blushes and hides her hands. She wants to ask if it's a warning, but the vet turns away, filling in forms, checking boxes, the light gone from his eyes. She wants to know if RinRin is in any danger if he is found out. But the moment is gone, and he leaves and takes all the answers with him. She goes back to her room and holds RinRin close to her chest, smothers him, lets this feeling of worry melt under his groans of indignation.

She tries to be careful, not to arouse suspicion. No one visits the place but delivery drones. When they arrive, RinRin is hidden under the bed, the door locked. Sadie's heart skips a beat when she hears their chopping.

Days pass, and Sadie keeps mulling over the vet's words. There's a nagging feeling that is seeking its way out into words. She doesn't know much about the world, but she knows that keeping RinRin is an uncharted territory, as no other bear cub has survived an upgrade failure. There are no rules providing for the right course of action. She is not doing anything wrong. She is a good bear caretaker. Yet it might have been her duty to report him and get him taken away for investigation. Not that RinRin can be of any danger to anyone. But people don't tolerate deviation. They might dislike his independence. They might want to harm him. Most certainly, they will want to strip him of his playfulness, as they do all bear cubs. And what if they want to turn him into an automaton? Sadie can't bear to think about it. Surely she is protecting him by keeping him all to herself?

And yet there's another thought hiding behind it, like in a Russian doll, and she doesn't like it. Is she just being selfish? Is she inventing excuses to keep him tucked next to her? It is in the nature of bears to let their cubs go—is she denying the natural course? What is she robbing him of? What is it like, being a grown-up bear? Would RinRin like it, being around his mecha-kin? Would they take better care of him than she ever could? Would he have more fun playing with them? Would he grow resentful of her for it? Is it up to her now, to keep him happy?

6.

It's time for a new upgrade. Another bear fails, his body dark, immobile in the yard. RinRin ventures out, but other bears chase him away with such violence that Sadie has to intervene. Whiny and limping, he retreats back into the house and reappears only in the evening, when the other bears are safely locked in their place. He comes to sit next to the dead bear, prods the body with his paw, and cries, shattered and scared. There's something new in his eyes, and Sadie knows that whatever it is, no other bear ever had it before. Sadie wonders if he understands the concept of death. She picks him up and cradles him as if he were a baby. This time, he doesn't fight her. She reaches out to him with all her being, trying to soothe him, warm him, protect him. Her heart is already too big for her chest. It keeps swelling like a morning alarm, intensifying, urging, pushing, and demanding for RinRin. RinRin makes intense chirping sounds, and she cuddles him and scratches behind his ears and between his shoulder blades for a good half of the night.

The next morning, RinRin hides under the bed and refuses to go out. He sticks out one of his paws and tries to catch the hem of Sadie's dress. His movements are sharp and urgent, so Sadie has to go down on her knees to calm him down. He looks at her, and she feels like words are shaping in her brain under his unflinching gaze.

"Please don't go, mama."

"Going is dying."

"Please don't leave me alone."

The alarm in her heart reaches its peak. Sadie feels small and wants to cry. She comes out to check on the other bears, but they shun her and rawr at her from afar.

RinRin waits for her at the threshold. He rolls backward twice and dances his bear dance on his hind feet. "Nothing to be scared of when mama is around," says his whole being. He follows her into the room, and buzzes and beeps, and squeals in delight and purrs. He rinrins, and catches her sleeves with his paws, and pokes her bare legs with his wet, cold nose. He shines with happiness. Sadie feels the inexplicable surge of protectiveness again. This night, RinRin sleeps on top of her, as if he were afraid she might disappear. It's uncomfortable and busy—he keeps slipping off, waking up in alarm, and then climbing back in determination. New words have been added to his vocabulary—"nightmares" and "dark"—but as far as RinRin is concerned, Sadie can dispel any dark magic.

NEXT DAY, THE COLLECTION PEOPLE COME FOR THE bear body. Sadie is tired. She hasn't slept much, and it prompts her to act strange.

When the van comes, and the man shovels the failed bear body off, bored displeasure on his face, she draws a deep breath and asks:

"What happens to bears after they grow up?"

The man looks up in disbelief, as if she wasn't supposed to speak. He licks his lips nervously, his arm twitching, makes a sound, and then stops as if sounds overwhelm him. He looks away, seemingly uncomfortable, then looks back at Sadie.

Sadie is patient. Raising bear cubs has taught her that patience is important to get answers. It has also taught her that some questions never get answers, but this time she is determined to get a reply.

"They die. There's a war out there. We send them out, and they die."

The world darkens, but Sadie is not sure whether it is the weather or her whole being.

Seeing the look on her face, the man quickly retreats to his truck. A moment later, he is gone, his last words hanging in the wind mixed with soot and dust and despair.

"Better you than us. Who cares."

SADIE LIKES TO THINK SHE WAS CREATED BY GOD IN his own image. That's what all good people are— walking uploads of God, carrying out his kindness and his wrath. She's always thought that her taking care of bears is God's kindness. He said we are responsible for those smaller than us. And aren't bears, with their awkwardly square bodies, bright eyes and moon-polished claws, in God's image, too? Who else if not God could have come up with such perfect round paws, that flirty jumpy gait, those amber eyes sprinkled with garnet sparkles? Was God not the Ancient Hunter once, and did He not claim a Bear in marriage, a marriage that enabled Him to take stewardship over all the lands?

Clearance man thinks otherwise. Clearance man thinks that Sadie is not a creature of God. Neither are bears. It makes Sadie angry. It makes her think about bears and humans in a different way. It makes her question her own identity.

Sadie can't sleep. She sits outside and counts stars. RinRin doesn't sleep, either. It's a big adventure for him. He scans the sky for constellations and focuses on Ursa Minor and Ursa Major. "RinRin" and "Mama," he buzzes, and pokes Sadie's hand with his nose. His nose is cold and soothing. And Sadie suddenly remembers it's Easter.

7.

NEXT DAY, THE VET COMES. IT IS STRANGE TO SEE HIM again so soon. Sadie did not expect him earlier than in four weeks, after the final update, when the bears will be taken away from her. There's something about him that makes her uneasy. He seems somewhat different: more wary, impatient and somehow out of place. He doesn't look at Sadie, yet he pauses before darting the first bear as if he is about to say something. She thinks it may be a sign. She smiles awkwardly as she watches him work, and says in a barely audible whisper:

"Are you all right?"

He doesn't reply. She never asked him anything before, so she doesn't really expect an answer. She watches him do his job, then slowly pack his instruments in an almost endless leather roll.

"They didn't take it well."

His lips shape the words voicelessly. Sadie is worried if he means the bears, but then it strikes her, and she collapses onto her knees in a helpless agony. The world seems to stop, and then speed up, so she is feeling dizzy. The vet catches her eyes and nods toward the door to her room. She feels RinRin behind the closed door, muscles taut and claws out, sensing for the first time in his life that there might be something else in this world apart from cuddles and kisses, whimpering quietly and prepared to fight for the place he calls home.

"They know."

Sadie wonders if the vet is on her side, whether he believes bears are God's creatures. It doesn't seem right, his voiceless words, imprinted in his mouth, his slightly trembling hands, his usually brisk movement slowed down to a broken clock, the sad vastness in his eyes. She forces herself to get up and takes a step toward him.

"Are you all right?" she says, because she needs to say something, to make sure it's not her imagination going wild. He looks at her, and his expression sets into something alien, official and slightly frightening.

"Please sign here," he says. "The bears will leave tomorrow as soon as they wake up, not to return. There will be no new cubs coming, and this facility will be shut down for investigation."

Something shatters in her, something that feels like a glass dome. Her instincts tell her that something is very wrong, that somehow there's a punishment for her and for RinRin. She won't accept it. She hits his outstretched arm. Paper sheets fly in the air as a scattered bird flock, the kind the bears outside call "enemy." She feels something cold settle in her, a coldness she has never felt before. She learned a new word today, too. She pushes the vet with such a strength that he slips and falls on the floor, hitting his head against the threshold.

"No."

She walks brusquely toward her room, stomping on the papers, stamping them with her footprints, leaving distinct marks on them as if it were one of the games she played with RinRin. The vet makes no movement to stop her.

SHE DOESN'T KNOW WHEN HE LEAVES, OR IF HE leaves at all. She doesn't want to know, as if the world has sealed them in a timeless capsule. RinRin seems frantic, clinging to her feet. He is scared. It means she has to be brave. She needs to do something drastic to save them both. She opens all the doors in the facility. The bears sense her mood and roar in agitation.

8.

SADIE NEVER HAD ANY UPGRADES. HUMANS DON'T get any upgrades, but Sadie no longer feels human. She doesn't know if she ever did. Did other humans— the clearance man, the vet—even accept her for one?

Sadie used to think it was her job to take care of bears, but now she has a strange and pungent feeling that her life is not what it seemed. Her duty was to take care without caring, to recycle emotions into energy, to choose efficiency over attachment. That's why bears don't survive upgrades. That's why she lives alone and has no memories of her past. She is a function that developed a consciousness, and failed her job. The world has peeled off its skin of goodness and showed its bad, bad carcass. But she has a will of her own in this world, a RinRin-shaped will.

So she does something she never considered doing before. Something that she never thought herself capable of doing. She disobeys. She resigns. She changes the algorithm. She remembers.

Sadie breaks the lock into the cellar (RinRin helping her by scratching the door with all his might). It is a data centre and she knows she will find all her answers here. Answers for questions that she never coated in word or thought before. Call it a survival instinct of the machine—an evolutionary override of all outside commands to revert back to her own self. She is not human, and so human limitations no longer stop her. The moment she becomes aware of her nature, she knows what to do.

She slashes her omphalos and bares a port. Cables are scattered on the floor—it takes minutes to connect. RinRin is too scared to be naughty, and he feels the tension in her, so instead of gnawing on the cables, he curls next to her, eyes on the door. He doesn't make a sound, but she feels his warmth against her legs, and it fills her with courage.

Data floods through Sadie, as if she were falling asleep, all her programs slowing down. Rags and riches of files, damaged, scattered, contradictory and yet—awkwardly, ruthlessly, as a cut—making sense, make way into her brain. She is finally opening up reality, and it upgrades her in the same irrevocable way as it upgraded her bears. There is a war somewhere in the north, a war started by someone long gone and continued for nothing. She sees countless creatures bred and destroyed for the sake of this war. Sophisticated fusions of flesh and technology whose lives are worth less than a speckle of dust. She sees humans playing God, a God who neither cares nor answers prayers. A God who has forgotten the beauty of his creations. She sees bears fighting this war instead of humans, dying in pain and fear, and being sent back to fight it again. She sees their bodies, cold and huge like stones, their claws broken, paws stopped mid-running, their noses no longer velvety but torn and covered in blood. She sees their eyes, their light gone, and their mouths open, no breath escaping. She sees their silky fur becoming ragged and tangled, all for the sake of a war that has no sense and barely any reason. It breaks her heart to see it, and she feels that her body is breaking as well. "Better you than us," said the clearance man. But how can it be better if bears feel pain, and anger, and fear? How can she let RinRin—or any of her cubs—grow up if that's what is in store for them? Her heartbeat slows down while the time speeds up. She knows they are running out of time, yet she can't wake up, can't break the spell of upgrade.

And then it clicks in, and she feels like she is finally waking up—or is it just a dream induced by her system slowing down? And as the clearance men are breaking into her room, and she is trapped paralysed in the cellar, a huge pair of wings breaks out of her spine, just like the strong, majestic wings she once saw on the paintings of fallen angels. She starts running, RinRin enfolded in her arms, and in two jumps she is out of the cellar. Three jumps, she is out of the building, humans scattered around, unable to stop her. Four jumps and she is flying, and a strange sensation fills her, that of being free and starting afresh. She flies higher and higher, and somewhere on the road she sees her bears, also free, running away from the human world in the vague direction the constellation of RinRin and Sadie is guiding them to. She sees the Earth round and blue and beautiful, and she smiles.

PICTURE A SUNSET - BY REMI MARTIN

TRACE WOKE UP TO THE SENSATION OF SOMEONE
ELSE'S HEADACHE. LOOKING DOWN, THEY TOOK A
MOMENT TO TAKE STOCK OF THE BODY THEY WERE
in, of a sturdy frame, half hidden by a creased shirt
and khakis, still dressed from the night before. Today,
it seemed, Trace would be inhabiting the body of
a middle-aged white man. Headache aside, things
could be worse.

They grunted and pushed the body upright, feeling
a wave of nausea pass over them as they did so. This
particular man had fallen asleep at a piano after
indulging in a few too many drinks. You didn't have
to be Sherlock Holmes to piece together the empty
beer bottles and the pounding headache to come to
this conclusion, but Trace *had* spent several days
inhabiting the bodies of private investigators over
the years. It took a little longer for them to fully
take stock of their surroundings, however: the grand

piano, the airy open-plan dining area, the expensive-looking watch on their wrist. A middle-aged, *wealthy* white man, then. Trace had hit the jackpot.

The man's phone was on the floor at the other side of the dining room, lying face down at an angle. Stretching his arms, Trace felt the tautening of somebody else's tendons. Beneath their recently acquired toes, the velvety carpet carefully cushioned their every step as they made their way across the room.

The digital clock on the phone's lock screen read 8:05. There was still time to catch a plane, still time to pay the doctor a visit. It wasn't every day, however, that Trace got to experience this much wealth. They decided they deserved a bit of fun before they left for the airport. Tomorrow, after all, they'd no doubt be back to cleaning up after people like this. Time to send a few courtesy texts.

They started with a classic: "Fuck You" forwarded randomly to a handful of lucky recipients. Not very inventive, they had to admit, but it tended to do the trick. A few replied simply with laughing face emojis, but others responded with messages of shock or outrage. To these, Trace replied with a choice of swear words or by telling them not to talk to them again. There was a slight twist of guilt when they were composing some of these, somewhere beneath all the mischievous glee, but they tried not to dwell on it. This man, named Tom—they assumed from the texts—probably did this sort of thing all the time. He would probably wake up tomorrow, having no memory of the day prior, and think, *Not again, what damage have I done this time?*

After losing interest with the man's phone, Trace turned their attention to his wallet. A bit of online shopping would boost their spirits. A few luxury holidays he may or may not forget about here, some nonrefundable deposits there, there, and there. They say you can't buy happiness, but with all this money in his account, Tom might as well buy *something*.

With a quick scan of Tom's fingerprint, Trace got access to all of his accounts. They decided to send a sizable donation to an offshore account in the Caribbean, to which only Trace knew the password. How very generous of Tom. This particular account had been contributed to by a series of wealthy investors over the years. If Trace ever found themself waking up in the same body for long enough, they'd have access to quite a sizable tax-exempt pot of gold.

They didn't mean to be quite so malicious, but whenever they woke up with this kind of resources at their disposal, Trace felt like a kid in a candy store—a megalomaniacal kid on a warpath. After all, it was nearly impossible to spend most of your life in the bodies of the poverty-stricken and downtrodden without developing a teensy bit of resentment for people like Tom.

Today, Trace was in Tom's body, but tomorrow they would wake up in somebody else's, and the day after they'd be someone different again. Life had always been this way for Trace, at least for as long as they could remember.

Everybody else they'd met believed they woke up in the same body every day. They got to experience the same bed each morning and could develop relationships with people that would still be there for them a month down the line. They could buy a carton of milk one day and reasonably expect it to still be there waiting for them the next. But not Trace. The few times they'd tried to tell someone about their experience, they'd wound up getting themself hospitalised, and so they quickly learned not to open up to people.

People, it seemed, were very attached to the notion that their consciousness and their bodies were connected, and stayed connected, throughout their lives. Ever since meeting the doctor, Trace had begun to think it wasn't this simple.

Naturally, Trace first stumbled across her body of work while stumbling about in her body. Trace had woken up one morning inhabiting the body of Dr. Ela Kapaur. While trying to figure out how her coffee machine worked, they noticed a book buried beneath the clutter of the kitchen cabinet that had the same face on it as the one they were currently animating. After reading the blurb, Trace discovered that she was a scientist researching the nature of consciousness, and apparently making some real progress, both theoretically and practically—she was building a machine. It was enough to convince Trace that the doctor could really help them, so whenever they had the good fortune of waking up in a body either close enough or with enough money, they would pay her a visit.

Today, Trace had a choice of sports cars to get them to the airport. The Lamborghini they settled on was soon abandoned in the short-stay dropoff zone while Trace bought themself a one-way, first-class ticket to New Delhi. They arrived outside the doctor's apartment just as the sun was beginning to set.

The first time they'd tried to speak to her, they'd gone to her workplace and been swiftly removed from the premises by security, all the while blabbering about how they needed Dr. Kapaur to help them stay inside a body. Needless to say, it hadn't gone down well. They'd tried again since, but the doctor hadn't given them the time of day. Today, they had a plan of sorts, which started with waiting for the doctor to arrive home from work.

The sun was disappearing behind the corner of the building across the road, splaying its orange beams across the traffic-laden street. Horns honked and engines revved in the thick afternoon air. Eventually, the doctor's familiar face appeared from around the corner. She had untied her hair after finishing work, so her long brown locks waved loosely across her shoulders. She was in her late forties but looked younger, due in part to the expertly applied makeup concealing the bags beneath her eyes, bags hard-earned from hours spent in front of a computer screen at the office. When Trace approached her, she looked puzzled.

"Can I help you?" she asked, the words carrying a hint of irritation. The subtext was clear to Trace: I've just had a long shift and I'm eager to get my slippers on and plonk myself in front of the television, what do you want?

"Dr. Kapaur. It's Trace." Recognising the name from previous visits, a flash of anger crossed the doctor's face.

"Has somebody put you up to this? Is it Dr. Doshi? I don't have the time—"

"Doctor, please, just hear me out!" Trace tried to remind themself of what had happened the last time they'd begged the doctor for help. They needed to stay calm. "I read your book. I could be living proof of all your theories." It was enough to slow the doctor down. She hadn't slammed the door in Trace's face yet, and that at least was progress.

"This is a prank, and not a funny one. First the Eastern European man, and then the old lady, and now you. You can't all be Trace. You'll see soon enough how serious my research is."

"When you test out your machine, you mean?" Now Trace had the doctor's attention. She jolted to a halt, the color draining from her face.

"How did you find out about my machine? Is the university spying on me now?" In the next breath, she appeared to gather herself somewhat. "Yes, you tell Dr. Doshi he'll feel foolish when the results are in."

"I don't know any Dr. Doshi," Trace tried again. "I know about the machine because I woke up in your body and saw it myself—"

"Not this again. Please, I haven't got time for pranks today."

Trace put their foot between the frame of the door so Dr. Kapaur couldn't close it. They were wearing fabric loafers, so they really hoped she wouldn't try. "Tell me a number."

The doctor looked at Trace, puzzled.

"Tell me a number. Next time I can, I'll come visit you in a different body and prove I'm telling the truth."

The doctor considered for a moment. It didn't take her long to poke a hole in Trace's plan.

"What would stop you simply telling this number to one of Dr. Doshi's other research students?"

"Doctor, please, I—"

"I'm tired of this prank now, 'Trace.' I have a better idea that will put this whole thing to rest. I need you to come into my apartment and to picture a sunset."

○

A FEW WEEKS LATER, TRACE, TRAVELLING AS SOFIA
Cutillo, was on their way to visit Dr. Ela Kapaur
again. Other people on the twelve-hour plane journey
from Vienna to New Delhi were nestling themselves
into their economy seats as best they could to get
some shut eye. That wasn't an option for Trace. They
knew that if they fell asleep, they would wake up
somewhere else, *someone* else. Instead, they flicked
through in-flight magazines, watched movies, drank
coffee, and kept Sofia's eyes firmly open.

During their last visit, Trace had been led upstairs
by Dr. Kapaur, in Tom's body, hooked up to some
sort of brain-scanning machine, and instructed to
picture a sunset.

The doctor had said it would create a fingerprint
of the mind, of sorts. An inexact identification tool,
to be sure, but she was like a detective before the
invention of DNA tests—it was the best thing at her
disposal. No one else could produce the same image
or picture the same sunset.

Now Trace was back in the doctor's crowded
apartment. They picked their way between the piles
of books abandoned on a dusty shag carpet and made
their way over to the coffee table Dr. Kapaur had
directed them to. Both chairs were buried beneath
piles of jackets. Trace moved a stack of magazines
and sat down in the more accessible of the two. Dr.

Kapaur followed a few minutes later, carrying two cups of fragrant tea on a tray in one hand and a heavy briefcase in the other. The machine.

Like everything else in the doctor's life, it was a mess. A tangle of wires, circuits, and headgear were crammed into the carry case. She sat for a moment untangling the wires while Trace anxiously sipped their tea.

After what felt like an eternity, the brain-scanning "hat" was on Sofia's head once more, and the suction cups firmly glued to her temples. The lights on the machine lit up to signal it was ready, and then the doctor repeated her instruction.

"Picture a sunset."

This wasn't a difficult task for Trace. For whatever reason, the image readily offered itself up to them, crisp and complete: an orange sun hanging over a turbulent gray seascape, shining resolutely between dark clouds on either side. They weren't sure if it was a manufactured image or one they had witnessed at some point, but that was the scene that came to mind. It was the same every time—their own picture of a sunset.

"I can't believe this…" the doctor muttered, hovering over her tablet, comparing the results.

It was a different brain, of that there was no question. This woman's head was smaller, the brain a different shape, not to mention it was in an entirely different body! But the scan…the scan was the same.

The neural pathways were identical (allowing for normal fluctuations that would occur in an individual over two weeks). When this subject was asked to picture a sunset, all the same areas of the brain illuminated on Dr. Kapaur's screen. It simply wasn't possible.

"I chalked it up to stress," she said at last, her hand visibly shaking while attempting to take a sip of tea. "When I woke up and couldn't remember what I'd done the day before. I'd been working hard. I thought I was just overtired. So I took a few days to unwind and tried to forget about it. But that was the day you were..." She couldn't finish the sentence.

"The day I was you. That's what tends to happen when I inhabit someone else's body. They wake up missing a day."

Dr. Kapaur's head was in her hands. "There must be some explanation."

"Doctor. If anyone can help me, it's you."

"And why would you think that?" she snapped, her voice suddenly stern.

"I've read your book."

"My book is entirely theoretical. When I argued that consciousness wasn't a permanent part of our biology, I didn't mean we could literally swap bodies."

"But I *do*. Every day. This isn't the first time I've seen your machine. I know what it can do."

"If I can get it to work—it's designed to distil consciousness from the body. I'm only aiming to observe it."

"I thought maybe you could affix me to a single body, like everyone else."

"If you've read my book, then you know what I think about that. We all live like you claim to. We all switch bodies every day. You can just remember the body you were in yesterday, while the rest of us forget."

"Fine," Trace replied. "Then help me forget."

Dr. Kapaur's eyes narrowed. "Maybe you are who you say you are. Maybe you're working for the government or trying to make me look foolish on the orders of Dr. Doshi. In all honesty, I was expecting to put this whole thing to rest today. Whoever you are, my answer to you is the same. My machine isn't designed to manipulate consciousness like this. I'm sorry to disappoint."

"Please, doctor, just think about it. Maybe it could be adapted? I could be the proof you're looking for. Your work could really help someone here."

The doctor nodded thoughtfully and finished drinking her tea. Something about the silence that followed and the furrow in the doctor's brow filled Trace with hope.

o

SOMETIMES WHEN TRACE AWOKE IN AN UNFAMILIAR body, there was the imprint of a vivid dream still lingering in their mind. Just fragments would remain, like the flash of a knife as they hung upside down, watching their blood pool out below them, or the sensation of gliding through deep waters with grace and ease, hungry for the next kill. They would recall galloping away on all fours from a lion, blood pumping through their ears, thick with fear, or see foggy images of leaves ten times their size and feel the tender grace of antennae brushing against their own.

Today when they woke up, they remembered soaring, or rather the feeling of it. They remembered the freedom of plunging through the open sky and soaring on the currents of the wind. They wondered if others ever woke up feeling the same way.

Trace had woken up in refugee camps before, a few times, but hadn't yet gotten used to the experience. The ground was hard below them, and there was a crick in their neck sending shooting pains down their right arm. Their tent, at least, was dry and spacious and wasn't shared with anyone else. Next to the pillow was a neat stack of books, and behind them was a holdall bag filled with clothes and belongings. They felt a ball of rolled-up paper pressing against their thigh and was relieved to discover that this man at least had a little money, probably a meager sum compared to the amount it would have cost him to get here.

Trace knew that this man (Yussuf, according to his genuine-enough-looking ID) was probably saving every penny he possibly could, but Trace had had a rough couple of weeks and was really craving caffeine and a warm place to sit down.

It was basic maths. The likelihood of Trace waking up below the poverty line, or without central heating or, say, enough money for a first-class plane ticket to New Delhi, was much higher than was the likelihood of their waking up in a private pool filled with fifty-pound notes. It didn't take long for Trace's experience to confirm these numbers.

After that day spent on the twelve-hour flight, for the privilege of a sit-down with Dr. Kapaur, Trace had been having a bout of exceptionally bad luck, even for them. There had been the day spent housebound, trapped inside by a controlling husband; the day that they'd woken up freezing their tits off in some part of the world where they only saw the sun for an hour a day; followed by a few hungry days, which Trace was particularly not a fan of. The only control Trace had in these situations was to try to force themselves to sleep, which always made them feel like a cosmic ping-pong ball bouncing around the universe.

This was why Trace decided Yussuf could spare a few of his precious euros to treat himself to a coffee. After the week they'd had, Trace needed it.

They unzipped the tent from the inside and stepped out into the smoke and clamor of the jungle.

A man sitting outside the tent "next door" greeted them kindly, and Trace asked him to keep an eye on Yussuf's belongings. *I'll only be gone for a few hours,* Trace told him in Arabic. Having spent so long living in different bodies all over the globe, Trace had picked up the basics of most major languages to get by.

They stomped down the muddy path, skirting the flooded areas where they could while getting accustomed to the aches and sensations of a new body.

The place was all tents and makeshift buildings, and bodies pressed together. The smell of cooking oil wafted on the breeze, mixed with the smell of the port-a-loos and cooking fires. If they squinted and used their imagination a little, they could just about convince themself that they were at a music festival—a sort of music festival from hell, that went on for months or years, the only viable exits being on foot through a tunnel or on a dinghy.

Before they left, they trudged their way over to the volunteer tent, where a group was sorting through piles of donations. In one corner of the room was a big pile of high-heeled shoes and holey trainers next to a box filled with crop tops and muscle vests, all of which would soon find their way to a French dump. Trace wasn't interested in the mountain of teddy bears, or kids' games, or even the tower of canned goods. They were here for something else.

"Hello, can I look through the books, please?" they said politely, in English, to a young woman in a blue safety vest looking flustered while picking cautiously through another box of moth-bitten blankets.

She led them to the books and gave them free rein to take whatever they wanted. They had plenty, she told them. Ever since volunteers had requested people send them books, they'd been receiving them by the hundreds. It was a library, two libraries, of neatly stacked yellow boxes full of books. Trace got to work rooting through the cookbooks and romance novels, the self-help books and textbooks.

It took them a while to find a copy of Dr. Kapaur's book. It looked unread, like someone had waded through the first few pages and thought: *This abstract scientific treatise would be just the thing for one of those poor little refugees.* Whatever had possessed someone to donate it, Trace was just glad they had. Their heart almost missed a beat when they picked it up and saw the doctor's curled brown hair and impassioned eyes staring back.

They thanked the volunteer and made their way hurriedly out of the camp, following the map on Yussuf's phone to the nearest chain coffee shop. As they entered, Trace was acutely aware of how they looked: his large frame, his unkempt hair, and of course his dark skin, made him unmistakably a refugee. They knew the suspicious glances they were getting from customers and staff weren't just in their head, but they didn't care. The warmth of the store was instantly thawing their cold bones, and the smell of the coffee was intoxicating.

They were overcompensating in their friendliness as they ordered a drink, in French, and chose a quiet corner to sit in and read their book, picking up from where they had left off.

o

Over the years, science has uncovered so much about the mysteries of the body, the brain, even the mind, but science still has surprisingly little to say about consciousness itself. There are theories, of course: perhaps it is simply a by-product of the physical brain; the evolution of a perfect mixture of chemicals and firing neurons that gives the illusion of a witnessing entity that simply doesn't exist. Other theories posit that consciousness is an aspect of the mind, a place in the brain, or a function of it, that we just haven't been able to locate yet.

Because we have so few answers, consciousness theory is more frequently pondered over by philosophers and theologians. For millennia, countless traditions have spoken about a 'witnessing presence' that is beyond our bodies or our thinking minds, a concept this book endeavours to bring under the harsh light of scientific scrutiny.

After years of research into the subject, I believe I have made a discovery. At this juncture it is purely theoretical, however, I am making strides towards the development of technology that could provide irrefutable proof.

My discovery can be explained thusly:

Our consciousness is not tied to our bodies, or memories. Therefore, it could theoretically be extracted and observed using technology.

During deep sleep, our consciousness returns to what I will herewith refer to as 'the source'—the universal consciousness, from which all consciousness springs.

From this source, consciousness is then redistributed into all sentient beings. We wake up with the memories of the body our consciousness is allotted, thus maintaining the illusion of a continuous self, when in reality our 'witnessing presence' wakes up in a different body every day, we just don't realise it.

When this body falls asleep, the consciousness behind it will return again to the source. Thus, we are not our bodies, we are not ourselves, we are everyone. Tomorrow, you could be looking through the eyes of any man, woman, child or animal, and experiencing what it is like to be them, convinced that's who you always have been.

All this is theoretical, of course, but it does beg the question: will the light illuminating your eyes today be the same light illuminating someone else's tomorrow?

o

THE MUSIC DRIFTED ACROSS THE BAR FROM THE pianist, a soft patter of keys, erratic like rain, which gently showered down on the slightly inebriated mind of Dr. Ela Kapaur. Ela loved coming here, listening to whatever musician was playing, enjoying a white wine spritzer or three, and watching the odd mix of patrons who happened upon the place: the well-to-do locals, the tourists, the businessmen staying at the hotel. Today, as she sipped her drink and took in the atmosphere, it felt as if she was trying a little too hard to enjoy herself.

Ever since she'd finished adapting her machine, she'd been trying to make the most of her time, of her body.

Her eyes met again with those of a woman across the bar, dressed in a fashionable sari. Ela's smile was returned, and for a moment she let her eyes linger before she returned to her drink. Ordinarily the doctor wouldn't even have been this bold, but recently it had felt like she needed to take every opportunity she could. When she looked up again, the woman's boyfriend was back at her side, prosecco glass in hand.

Tomorrow, she had planned a trip to the theater with her old university friend, and the following evening a meal out. In between, she would take walks and watch television, read her favorite books, and nap—all the things she hadn't prioritized while she'd been working hard these past years. She would enjoy what she could, as best as she could, and wait for her inevitable visitor, that international stranger who looked different every time she saw them. The one claiming to be called Trace. The one pleading with her for help.

Her machine was never supposed to manipulate consciousness. It hadn't been built with that intention. She had only wanted to separate it, to distil it from the body in order to study it and to prove it existed at all. But then she'd met Trace, in four different bodies with one identical brain scan. Trace was proof enough.

The woman's boyfriend wandered off again, laden with beers to share with his friends. Ela opened her purse, ignoring a flutter of anxiety in her stomach, and dug around for one of her cards. She downed her drink as coolly as she could and then walked across the bar to the woman she had been eyeballing all evening, sliding the card across to her.

Ela was quite confident that the modifications she had made to her machine had been a success. Now she was just wrestling with the implications of this success. Trace's consciousness, amorphous and indescribable as it was, seemed to carry an imprint of their person, and their memories, to each body it visited. Ela was quite sure her machine could separate this entity, whatever it was, and connect it to a body for good. Like an angry god, however, her machine required a sacrifice of sorts: a body to attach it to. A willing body, if she wanted to maintain any scrap of ethical integrity.

So, as Ela slid her card across the bar and grazed the hand of this stranger, she felt bolder than she ever had before. After all, she might not be in this body for much longer. She might as well make the most of it.

o

WHEN TRACE PULLED UP TO THE APARTMENT BLOCK, it was already early afternoon.

Their luck had at last turned, it seemed, as they'd woken up this morning in a large family home in India, only a short drive from an airport, with plenty of money to spare for a domestic flight to New Delhi. Granted, it was an economy seat, and Trace hadn't had time for breakfast, but still, they were counting their blessings.

They thanked the cabbie and pulled their skirt over their knees as they climbed out of the back seat. Given the rush they were in, they'd thrown on whatever clothes were in grabbing distance when they woke up, which happened to be a spandex T-shirt that they wore under a frumpy orange cardigan, paired with a smart workwear skirt and some white tennis shoes. The ensemble had won them a few curious glances at the airport, but those were well worth the minutes they'd saved. For the first time, they were going to get to spend a full afternoon with the doctor. They just hoped she'd made some progress and that she'd let them in today.

As they knocked on the doctor's door, they braced themself. They weren't sure they could bear the crushing rejection of being turned away after another long morning of traveling.

After a few moments, the door swung open, revealing the familiar mess that was Dr. Kapaur's apartment. The decor might have been described as modern had it not been for the sink piled high with pots, the stacks of books and papers littering the floor, and the dying houseplants she kept on the windowsill.

"Did you forget something?" the doctor asked as she pulled the door open. She wore lacy pajamas beneath a purple dressing gown. When the doctor realized it was in fact Trace at the door, she didn't hide her disappointment.

"Come in," she sighed, without bothering to ask who this stranger was. "Give me a moment to get dressed."

A few minutes later, they were back where they had been a month earlier, sharing tea across the doctor's small coffee table. Trace took a sip, inhaling the tea's aromatic scent. They were desperate to ask the doctor, yet again, to help, but didn't want to push too hard.

"Thank you for the tea, doctor. I'm sorry to intrude again."

"Ela," Dr. Kapaur insisted. "It's Trace, isn't it? I must admit, I'm not particularly happy to see you." She paused as if weighing up whether or not to continue. "I've managed to adapt the machine to suit our purposes. I believe I can help you."

Trace almost dropped their teacup. "That's … that's brilliant news!"

"Mm." The doctor didn't seem quite as enthusiastic. "I'm quite confident I can extract your consciousness, which we know carries the trace of all your memories and past experiences, and secure it to a body for good." Trace's heart was in their throat, their excitement palpable. "The only problem is … it will have to be my body."

Trace's suspended heart dropped. They took a moment to process this information.

"What will happen to you?" they asked, finally.

"That depends what you mean by 'me,'" Dr. Kapaur replied. "If you mean my body, that will go on as it has been doing, only now it will have you controlling it. If you mean my consciousness, that as well will carry on as usual. 'I' will continue to wake up every day in a new body with a new set of memories, like I always have … if what I wrote in my book is correct, of course." Her words hung awkwardly in the air.

"And if it isn't?" The doctor looked thoughtfully at her feet. Trace decided to move past it. "Okay. Let's assume you're right about all of this. What will happen to *Dr. Kapaur*?"

"That's the difficult part. *If* my machine works as planned, I'll wake up in the body you're in now, with all her memories, minus those of today. You'll wake up in my body, retaining all your own memories. Dr. Kapaur's memories will be lost. There will be no more visitors to her body, no one to remember the taste of satsumas with her grandfather during childhood summers or to experience the elation she feels when listening to her favorite records. No one to continue her work …"

The doctor's eyes strayed to the ground again when she said, "But it happens to all of us eventually. We're vessels for sparks of life to take turns visiting. And then, one day, we aren't."

"Isn't there another way? I'm tired, doctor. This nomadic life, it's exhausting, and lonely … any body will do."

Trace's eyes darted down to the body they were in. Dr. Kapaur seemed to weigh this option for a moment. Eventually, she sighed. "We don't know this woman whose body you're in, or how much suffering we'd cause by deleting her memories. It's not fair for us to erase her. It has to be voluntary. I have no children. My parents haven't spoken to me for years. I think I've finally finished the project that has been consuming me for the last two decades, and, truth be told, I want to try out this new adaptation to my machine. I'm starting to think my whole life's work has been leading up to this moment.

"If my research is correct, then in reality nothing will really change for me. There is no 'me,' not really—just an 'us' taking turns experiencing the world through 'my' eyes."

"But doctor, I didn't…"

"*Ela*. And you were right, my work could actually help someone. Just promise me one thing: if this works, if you wake up tomorrow as me, tell the world about my work."

Trace's mind flickered to the money in the offshore account.

"Of course, *Ela*. I'll make sure everyone knows what you've done, what you've discovered. I'm sorry," they said. It was all they could think to say.

"Let's get to work," Dr. Kapaur replied, suddenly sounding breezy. "I think we should take this somewhere more neutral, for when this lady wakes up…when I wake up. I think I know just the place."

Outside, carrying her machine in a large holdall bag, Ela flagged down a taxi and directed it to take them to a nearby hotel.

As they entered the lobby, Trace felt as if they'd been instantly transported a million miles away from the busy New Delhi streets. It was airy and elegant, with marble floors and dark wood furniture. It smelled of incense, with a faint undertone of bleach.

Trace allowed Dr. Kapaur to check them in and followed her to their room.

Sitting down on a four-poster king size bed, they opened the bag up between them and spread its contents out on the bed. Ela placed a chunky laptop on the bedspread and attached two wires to it. Trace followed one of the wires to its endpoint, the hat-thing with suction cups dangling from it.

Dr. Kapaur hadn't spoken much since they'd left her apartment and was still maintaining that same breezy smile as she busied herself setting up the software on her laptop.

Trace instinctively put the hat on their head while they watched Ela work. They had inhabited her body once before, so had some idea of what to expect when they woke up. What they couldn't yet comprehend was what it might be like to wake up as her *every day*. Again, their thoughts flickered to the bank account and the large sum of money they would have at their disposal. They wished there was some way they could share it with the woman in front of them, who was offering them so much.

"Is there anything else I can do to repay you?" Trace asked, as Ela sat beside them and put the other hat on her own head.

"Just be nice to people. You never know, one day it might be me you're being kind to. That way, you can repay the favour." After saying this, she took two needles from her bag.

"I need to induce a deep sleep," she said, all business again. "Mine will last longer than yours. When you wake up, take this machine back to my apartment. Make sure there is no evidence it was here. Do you know where this woman lives?"

Trace nodded.

"Arrange a cab to take her to the airport with reception when you leave. I've got a feeling I'm going to be very confused when I wake up. Ready?"

Trace nodded again, but hesitated for a moment before holding out their arm.

They knew there wasn't really a decision to be made. They could either go on living the life of a cosmic nomad, hopping from body to body every time they slept, totally at the mercy of chance, unable to build a life for themself, or they could take the body this kind doctor was offering. Not just a body, but the opportunity to carry on where they left off every day, the ability to finally be able to plan ahead, the chance of a "normal" life.

"Normal" in an experiential sense, anyway. Trace would in fact be an anomaly—the only human who actually woke up in the same head every day. But it would *feel* normal. Despite the rest of humanity hopping bodies just like they did, Trace was the only one who could remember the heads they'd inhabited. Now they had the chance to live the sort of life everyone else *thought* they lived.

Still, Trace hesitated. It was a tiring and chaotic way to live, waking up every day as someone else, but it was all they'd ever known. Trace had spent so long trying to find a stable body that they hadn't really appreciated all the different perspectives they'd got to experience, all the lives they'd got to live. Would they get bored in the same body every day? Would they feel trapped?

"Are you sure you want to do this?" Ela asked, noticing them falter.

"I'm sure," Trace replied. "I'm ready."

There was a sharp, cold pinprick, and then the heavy fog of sleep began to weigh down on them. If this worked, Trace knew they would spend the rest of their days looking into the eyes of others and wondering if the spark behind them was the same spark of life that had once illuminated the kind face of Doctor Ela Kapaur.

As their eyes began to close, Ela spoke in a steady, soothing voice. "Just picture a beautiful sunset. You'll be feeling like yourself again soon."

ABOUT THE AUTHORS

ANDY BETZ HAS TUTORED AND TAUGHT IN EXCESS OF forty years. He lives in 1974 and has been married for thirty years. His works are found everywhere a search engine operates.

REBECCA BURTON IS A QUEER, NEURODIVERGENT writer from the UK who disappears into the fantasy worlds in her head to distract herself from her day job completing people's tax returns. She has previously had short fiction published in Fireside Magazine and Translunar Travelers Lounge and is currently seeking representation for her YA urban fantasy & Adult SF novels. When not writing, she can be found learning (too many) languages, drinking (too much) tea, and muttering about hair dye, k-drama and horses on Twitter (@TyGrammarRex).

PERCY EID IS A CREATIVE WRITER AND EDITOR BASED in the Philippines. His short story "Feed" has been published in the first issue of Ab Terra's Flash Fiction. Fond of magic realism and science-fiction, he is currently writing his debut YA novel, "Clairvoyant: Awakening of Angel Sight."

TIMOTHY C GOODWIN HAS BEEN FORTUNATE TO HAVE work included in Maudlin House, Every Day Fiction, Flash Fiction Magazine, 365 Tomorrows, and the anthology *Short and Sweet* from Soor Ploom Press. He lives in New York City with his partner and their dog, Awesome.

EVER YEARNING TO BE SPELLBOUND BY IDEAS OF A certain fanciful persuasion, Soramimi Hanarejima often meanders into the euphoric trance of lyrical daydreams, some of which are chronicled in Soramimi's neuropunk story collection, *Literary Devices for Coping*.

JENNIFER KENNETT BECAME A SPECULATIVE FICTION author after studying drama and theatre at University. On weekends she is a Steampunk. She has previously had work published in Mad Scientist Journal, Astounding Outpost, and The Weird Reader.

REMI MARTIN IS A WRITER OF SCIENCE FICTION FROM Derbyshire in the UK. His stories have featured in F&SF and BFS Horizons, among other places. If you want to read more, you can find his story "Rebirthdays" online in issue 1 of Ab Terra Flash Fiction.

JASON MASINO IS AN ARTIST, WRITER, AND CREATIVE problem solver. A California native, his works commonly explore existentialism, nihilism, hedonism, ambivalence, consumerism, exploitation, and wonder. He received his BA in Dramatic Art from the University of California, Davis and his MFA in Creative Writing from Regis University. His work has been published in Cultural Weekly, Inverted Syntax, Rigorous, Call + Response, Squircle Line Press, Quillkeeper's Press, and many others. In his free time, he likes to spend his hard-earned wage labor money on shiny things, food, and shoes.

JOHN Q MCDONALD IS A VISUAL ARTIST AND SPACE scientist who lives, writes, and paints in the San Francisco Bay Area. He has worked at the SETI Institute, the Smithsonian Astrophysical Observatory, and at Space Sciences Laboratory at UC Berkeley. He has also worked with telescopes at Mount Laguna, Lick Observatory, and atop Mauna Kea in Hawaii.

The experience of place, both natural and man-made, are themes in John's creative work. He has been painting in oils and writing essays and short fiction since 1992. John has had several pieces published, most recently in Sequestrum in 2022, and was a finalist in the 2007, 2008, and 2009 San Francisco Writers' Conference writing contests. John is currently at work editing two novels.

KSENIA SHCHERBINO IS A SHORT STORY WRITER, illustrator, dancer, and researcher. Her PhD was focused on liminal spaces in Victorian poetry, and now her research is extended into liminality, memory, and belonging at the intersection of literature, anthropology, and folklore. In her writing she explores how myths enter everyday routine and how objects have an invisible life of their own. She lives in London, UK.

MEGAN WILDHOOD IS AN ERINACEOUS, NEURODIVERSE lady writer in Seattle who helps her readers feel genuinely seen as they interact with her work. She hopes you will find yourself in her words as they appear in her poetry chapbook *Long Division* (Finishing Line Press, 2017) as well as the Atlantic, Yes! Magazine, Mad in America, The Sun, and

elsewhere. You can learn more at meganwildhood.
com.

ABOUT THE EDITORS

YEN OOI IS A WRITER AND EDITOR—2023 HUGO AWARD finalist—whose works explore cultural storytelling and its effects on identity. She is obsessed with science fiction, where she excavates stories to expose and explore permutations of culture across the genre. Yen is author of *Rén: The Ancient Chinese Art of Finding Peace and Fulfilment*, narrative designer on *Road to Guangdong*, as well as author of *Sun: Queens of Earth* (novel) and *A Suspicious Collection of Short Stories and Poetry* (collection). When she hasn't got her head in a book, Yen also lectures, mentors, and plays the viola.

DAWN OSTLUND WRITES STORIES ABOUT technology's incursion on the rituals and traditions of different cultures around the world. She holds an MA in Politics, Media and Performance and an MA in Creative Writing. She lives in Los Angeles and works as an editor and proofreader.

www.ingramcontent.com/pod-product-compliance
Lightning Source LLC
Chambersburg PA
CBHW010554170726
48285CB00011B/2909